# THE MULTIVERSE IS LEAKING

---

## BJ HYPES

First edition.

ISBN 978-1-7347586-0-3 (paperback)

ISBN 978-1-7347586-1-0 (ebook)

www.bjhypes.com

 Created with Vellum

# Preface

Due to the trustworthy nature of the British accent, it is recommended you read the following as such. To aid you in the process, a list of priming words has been compiled:

Tea, crisps, Manchester, Queen, guv'na, biscuits, trolly, jumper, kettle, & Richard the Third.

Further, it will help tremendously with my credibility if you imagine I'm a doctor. Not necessarily a medical professional, but please picture my name on a lovely certificate in a gold frame.

Since that's taken care of, it's only fair you know this entire book is a PSA to raise awareness about the most common cause of complete Multiverse collapse: not doing the dishes.

Across the Multiverse, all great events begin with one small act. In fact, we're usually only three wrong turns away from complete and utter obliteration, which is why you must do your dishes in a timely manner.

Luckily, there are many signs of collapse before implosion, but none so omnipresent and foreboding as a leak in the Multiverse. Should this happen, I recommend you find a large object, such as a bush or a rhinoceros, to hide behind so you may live out your time before collapse in peace.

Why do so many paths of unwashed dishes end in catastrophic annihilation? We shall see.

Sincerely,

BJ Hypes

# ONE

## Snacks

---

**K**ale could never find the remote. This may not seem like such an issue, but one minute he'd put it down on the table, and the next it would vanish. What furthered the oddity is that he'd often have to reach deep into the crevasses of the couch to find the remote, even though he always placed it on the table.

On average, it takes an oblivious human such as Kale 58 cycles of repetition to realize that something is amiss. This was the 57th cycle, and he was dangerously close to discovering what lay beneath his couch cushions.

But before Kale could prove his worth as an inquisitive and active protagonist, there was a quiet knock at the door. As he turned toward the sound, the entire door slammed forward with such force that the whole third-story apartment shook.

Standing there, boots smoking from the powerful kick, was a young man about Kale's age. His mane of hair was tied back by a bandana, and he slung an army-green duffel over his shoulder. He surveyed the narrow apartment and locked eyes with Kale.

"Snacks." The man held out his hand.

"In the cupboard." Kale looked around for the remote to quiet the TV, but couldn't find it.

"Nice to meet ya, *Intha Cupboard*. The name's Knightly. *Snacks* Knightly. I'm your new roommate." Snacks grabbed Kale's pointed finger and shook it. He dropped his duffel and propped the door back into place.

Kale was about to interject when he learned Snacks was phenomenal at speaking quickly.

"Sorry 'bout the door, I did knock. I've gotta thing about opening doors, so it's best if we just leave this slightly ajar. That's a funny idea, a jar for a door. Don't ya think, Intha?"

"Yes, but that's..."

Snacks pulled a wrench from his back pocket and gave a hearty whack to each of the hinges. "...There we go, good as new." Astonishingly, the door seemed to operate smoothly. In fact, it no longer made its usual squeaking sound.

"How did you—"

"—This room free? Yeah, it is." Snacks walked through the apartment with Kale in tow. There were three empty bedrooms. Thankfully, all of the doors were already open and Snacks just nudged them open a bit more with his elbow.

Snacks dragged his duffel to the doorway of the master bedroom and lifted it into Kale's hands. The surprising weight nearly knocked him over. Kale had no idea why he obeyed when Snacks asked him to hold down a stray lever on the bottom of the bag.

"How's the neighborhood? Do the coffee shops grind it fresh? Are the dinosaurs friendly?" Snacks unzipped a bit of the canvas and twiddled some knobs.

"Dinosaurs?"

Right at that moment, Snacks pulled a circular pin from the bottom of the bag. A loud ticking noise clicked through the apartment.

"Oh bother, is this one where they went extinct? I was really looking forward to visiting them. You know, the Goobasauras..." Snacks went on excitedly about dinosaurs while Kale nervously held the ticking bag. He frantically looked between it and Snacks as he tried, and failed, to get a word in.

"...And that's how it evolved to have the strongest sense of smell!" Snacks concluded as the ticking sped up considerably and the bag rumbled in Kale's hands. "Oh right," Snacks grabbed the duffel and tossed it into the master bedroom.

The moment it touched the ground, a blinding light burst from the bag with such power it slammed the door shut.

Snacks let out a heavy sigh and crouched down, "I hate opening doors." He wound a crank connected to his boot as a charged sound hummed from his feet. As Snacks took a kicking stance, Kale quickly opened the door in a desperate attempt to avoid annoying his neighbors any further.

Snacks smiled at him with admiration, but Kale was preoccupied with the room. Just seconds ago it had been completely bare, and now it was fully furnished. He could not contain a "Wow" as he stepped inside.

Assuming Kale's noise of admiration was in response to his earlier dinosaur facts, Snacks continued to list them off. Kale noted the Goobasauras was clearly Snacks' favorite.

The room felt like a 70s basement with wall-to-wall shag carpet and beanbag chairs. As Kale touched a lava lamp, and learned a Goobasauras had a twenty-foot wingspan, he remembered the many itching questions which burdened his noggin.

"You know, I'm very confused by...well, everything. Could you..." Kale turned around and Snacks was nowhere in sight, but there was the distinct sound of rummaging in the kitchen.

"I see the dishes are done...we're gonna get along just fine!" Snacks called out as the narrator nodded approvingly.

Kale absentmindedly approached the kitchen, believing that like eggs post-omelet, he had cracked.

"Oh, Intha, care for a soda?" Snacks said slyly as he poured a can of GeneriCola into a cup. Then he took his hands away, and the can stayed in place. It floated in the air and continued to pour.

So many thoughts, at least two or three, raced through Kale's mind that this took no priority.

Snacks smiled wide, expecting a similar response. "It blew my mind the first time I saw it too. I'm not supposed to reveal the secret, but here..." Snacks beckoned Kale closer and pointed out that the soda can was, in fact, held up by a transparent piece of plastic.

As it is for many people, close-up magic was Kale's breaking point.

He let out the mightiest roar he could muster...and politely corrected Snacks that his name was not '*Intha*,' but '*Kale*.'

He was about to object and question further when Snacks interjected once more. "That's what I like about you, Kale. You're very easygoing."

It was the first compliment Kale had heard in a long time, and he very much liked it.

Perhaps coincidentally, perhaps not, across the Multiverse things shifted.

Snacks brought a few decorations to the living room, just a few lights and posters to cover the otherwise empty walls. Beyond a few barstools, the only nice piece of furniture Kale had was his couch, which the two promptly plopped down upon. Kale and Snacks began their epic bromance as many do, by mutually watching television...together.

Kale was particularly excited when Snacks presented his box set of *The Office* as he hadn't realized there were twenty seasons.

Snacks explained that he had borrowed this box set from Universe Kaleidoscope, which won "Best Universe" nearly 800 years in a row, beating out Universe No-More-Cancer (self-explanatory) and Universe Nuclear-Teddy-Bear (too long to explain). Universe Kaleidoscope's success was largely due to its continuation of *The Office* for an additional eleven seasons.

Throughout this, Kale nodded along politely. He assumed this was all a bit that had wooshed over his head.

After binging an entire season, Kale and Snacks needed a break, to process both emotions and food.

At that moment, Snacks reached for the remote and found it had vanished. As all sensible people do when something goes missing, he first checked within the couch cushions.

His hand reached down deep, farther than Kale believed the couch went.

"Huh," Snacks made a puzzled face. He tried to extract his shoulder-deep arm, but it didn't budge. "Hold on...just a...a little more..." Snacks ripped his arm out of the hole and proudly showcased his find. But rather than a remote, he held a can of soup.

Both puzzled at each other. Snacks inserted his arm again, retrieving yet another can of soup, and another, and another.

They stacked a small pyramid of tomato bisques and one clam chowder before Snacks finally found the remote.

He stared at Kale inquisitively. "Odd place to keep your soup, but I respect your desire for a firm couch."

Kale explained he hadn't purchased any soup, which prompted the two of them to finally remove the couch cushions.

They revealed crumbs, loose change, and a hole.

It was black and about the size of a grapefruit. Snacks' first instinct was to touch it. So he did. He reached inside and retrieved yet another can, crowning their soup pyramid. Kale hesitantly did the same and felt around inside some sort of empty wooden box.

The two pulled the couch away from the wall, but the hole followed. And though he was not a scientist, Kale definitively determined that the couch was far too small to contain a wooden box of this size.

"Hmmm. Must be a portal," Snacks said.

"A what?"

"A portal. You know, like a little door to another universe? Did you install it?"

Kale explained the couch had always just been there. It then dawned on him just how frequently he lost the remote.

"Ah, that makes sense. Objects do tend to gravitate toward portals."

Kale nodded along as if he understood. "Can we turn it off?"

Snacks retrieved the wrench from his back pocket and whacked the edge of the portal. Nothing happened. "Nope...but we can fill it so things will stop desiring to move toward it."

Snacks struggled to produce a huge bag of ping-pong balls from his jacket pocket. They most definitely could not have fit in such a small space, but at this point Kale was too overloaded with nonsense to comment.

Snacks placed a ping-pong ball in Kale's hands as he stood back and took shots. Alas, none of them went in.

Kale had never thrown anything well in his life, and yet his first attempt ricocheted off the ceiling, the television, the pyramid...and then landed squarely in the portal.

Scientists have yet to discover why we evolved this way, but when people sink trick shots, the excitement centers of their brain light up as if they took down an adult War Tortoise using only a boomerang.

Kale and Snacks could not contain their enthusiasm.

For the next few minutes, the two of them did trick shots into the portal. Kale learned his one talent in life was, apparently, throwing ping-pong balls into small holes. They continued until the portal over-flowed, and then Snacks taped over it with a sparkly, black material.

They put the cushions back, then high-fived regarding their success and their new collection of soup.

"You sure it's okay to just leave it?" Kale asked.

Snacks shrugged. "The simplest solution is often the easiest." He said it in such a profound tone that Kale didn't realize how little sense it actually made.

Just as they were about to start the eleventh season of *The Office*, there was a knock at the door. Because it was ajar, per Snacks' request, it slowly swung open.

Standing there was Kale's neighbor, Lonnie. She wore overalls covered in greasy fingerprints and held a thick flashlight. She walked in without waiting for a response: "Breaker."

Lonnie and Kale had met twice before. Both times, she had pushed her way into the apartment and flipped some switches on the fuse box. Despite having separate apartments, they shared a breaker.

"The name's Knightly. Snacks Knightly," he said as Lonnie breezed past him, not cold, but determined.

"Lonnie." She opened the fuse box and flipped switches in a rhythmic pattern, as if she was inputting a cheat code.

Kale always thought Lonnie looked tired, but one of the few social practices he knew taught him to keep that thought to himself.

"You look tired," Snacks commented.

Lonnie smiled groggily. "Thank you!" It was an eerily genuine and non-sarcastic response, which Kale knew because Snacks had taught him all about sarcasm just hours ago. "And that will do it." Lonnie flipped one last big switch and listened, her ears toward the door.

A small explosion from Lonnie's apartment across the hall caused

Kale to jump backward while Snacks and Lonnie stared at him curiously.

"You alright, bud?" Snacks asked.

Kale looked out into the hall and saw black smoke billow out of the open apartment. In a moment of bravery, or stupidity, he grabbed a fire extinguisher and rushed over.

There, he saw a humanoid figure engulfed in flames near the sink. He pointed and pulled the lever of the fire extinguisher, intending to put out whatever it was, but nothing happened.

Kale quickly read the instructions, pulled out a pin, turned a lever counterclockwise, and rubbed the side three times...only to look up and see the fire was gone.

Instead, there was a young woman in a long, tattered black cloak. She looked at him as though *he* was the one who had just been engulfed in flames.

"Is he always this jumpy?" Lonnie asked Snacks as the two appeared in the doorway behind him.

"Oh, I like him just the way he is." Snacks waved warmly to Kale, who was engaged in the act of bewildered word vomit. "Sound it out, buddy."

"Are you alright?" the woman in the black cloak reached out to touch Kale's forehead, then recoiled. "Oh, whoops. That could've been bad..." She promptly removed the ragged black cloak, revealing a flowery sundress. "I'm Del." She pressed a hand up against his forehead. Kale found her quite disarming without the cloak.

"Does he have scurvy?" Snacks asked genuinely.

Del touched a lot of Kale's face and pinched his cheeks. "He doesn't have a fever."

"Coffee?" Lonnie said at no one in particular.

Kale slumped down against the oven, "Sure?" He looked around for a coffee pot but didn't see one.

"Yes, Elonifred?" a feminine Australian brogue echoed above them.

Lonnie sighed. "Don't call me that. And run a diagnostic for craziness."

Suddenly, a huge robotic arm descended from the ceiling. At the tip of the arm was a big face made up of 64 pixels that smiled as they inched closer to Kale. "Hello. Please present your rear end for inspection."

"Coffee! Do I have to lower your humor threshold again?" Lonnie said sternly, as if she was a trainer reprimanding an inattentive walrus.

Coffee let out a long sigh as the robot face frowned. "Fine, Mom. Beep-boop, initiating boring medical procedures." Though the few pixels did not give Coffee much ability to convey it, Kale could feel the robot rolling its digital eyes. Two little arms sprung from the sides of the face and leached onto Kale's forehead.

"Hmmm...cancer...cancer...tumors...STIs...more cancer..." Coffee said as Kale's eyes got progressively wider. "...Yes, you're free of those. It's my diagnosis that you're...just bein' a weenie."

"Coffee..." Lonnie crossed her arms.

"I have one final test. Was this your card?" A third arm shot out from behind the face, holding a nine of diamonds.

"I...I don't..." Kale looked around as Lonnie slapped her forehead.

"I thought I removed all magician protocols from your system?! How do you keep doing that?" Lonnie trudged over to an old arcade cabinet in the corner of the room. She fiddled with the joystick and pushed buttons in rapid succession.

"A magician...never reveals...their secrets..." Coffee said as they powered down, the face barely able to keep its pixels open.

Snacks applauded.

"Well, looks like we're all set here. So...get out." Lonnie looked at the two of them as Snacks lifted Kale up. Kale took in the two opposing styles of the apartment. Along one wall, there sat a collection of tools and machines presented for most efficient access, while on another, there were bright colors and living things that sparked joy.

"Don't be absurd!" Del pulled out a large pot. "Stay for supper. I can't believe we've lived next to each other for months and never had a neighborly meal or board game night."

Snacks glanced at Lonnie. "Oh, we wouldn't want to impose..."

"Nah, stay." Lonnie kicked a piece of equipment lightly. "I'm just frustrated 'cause I can't get my gate working."

"Have you tried jiggling the handle? That usually works for me," Kale tried desperately to be helpful and rejoin the conversation.

Lonnie shook her head. "Tried that. It was working fine earlier, but since this afternoon...whatever. Let's just play *Cards Against Huge Manatees* and relax."

"It's mighty kind of you to make dinner." Snacks tipped an invisible hat at Del.

"It's no biggie, I'll just heat up some soup. Hope ya like tomato bisque!" Del opened a high cabinet and was immediately showered with hundreds of ping-pong balls, which filled the room. She chuckled a bit and looked at Lonnie curiously.

Kale weaved the events of the day together and turned to Snacks to share a laugh, but he had gone pale. His mouth was covered, and his eyes were wide.

"Snacks? What's wrong?"

Barely able to get the words out, Snacks took a few steps back.

"The Multiverse is leaking."

# TWO

# The Department of Multiverse Ventures

"Hello and thank you for calling the DMV. Due to our poor planning and inability to listen to low-level employees who, by living through inefficiencies, understand the easiest way to fix them, there is currently a huge wait time. Please stay on the line, or go f\*\*k yourselves. We really don't care..." Snacks held up his phone as the cheerful automated voice spread through the otherwise tense apartment.

Lonnie flicked a rubber band on her wrist as she examined the hole. Suddenly, Del's hand popped through and grabbed Lonnie. Del's laughter rang out from the other apartment as she returned, her dress now used to carry cans of soup.

"This is no laughing matter, Del." Lonnie swabbed the inside of the portal and brought the sample over to the arcade cabinet.

Del waved her off and opened a few cans of soup. "A little death never hurt anyone."

Kale's eyes went wide. "Not to sound like a broken repeater, but could someone, anyone, explain what's going on? We saw the portal in our home earlier. What's changed?"

"I thought that portal led to another universe, not our own." Snacks paced as he held the phone up to his ear.

Lonnie didn't look up. "Didn't you learn about this in Multiverse

Basics? Portals like this don't appear in the same universe." She slammed buttons on the arcade cabinet, then suddenly stopped. "Damn...this tests positive for leakage residue."

"You can relax," Del said warmly to Kale. "It'll all be fine in the end."

For someone who had been engulfed in flames earlier, Kale found her composure comforting.

"As much as I love and cherish Del..." Lonnie started. "Because of her work, she doesn't exactly know when to be terrified anymore."

"Oh, what do you do?" Snacks asked, his hand over the receiver.

"I kill people!" Del said with enthusiasm. Snacks nodded knowingly while Kale took a step back. Del handed him a business card.

It was all black other than big letters at the top that said, *"Reapr–Death Comes For Us All, Why Not Make It Easier?"* On the back was her name and title: *"Del–Project Coordinator of F.O.D.–Coconut Division."*

"So you're...a hitman? Hit-person? Assassin?" Kale asked nervously.

Del chuckled. "I just oversee F.O.D.s and make sure everything gets processed smoothly. Luckily, the app takes care of most of the work nowadays." Del held up her phone and demonstrated the app "Reapr." It had a hip minimalist design, and the intro animation showed silhouetted people being hit by cars or mauled by bears.

"F.O.D.s?" Kale asked expositionally.

"Falling Object Deaths. Specifically, my team works with those who die from falling coconuts. Did you know we kill more people each year than sharks?" Del excitedly explained some new features of the app, the body decay tracking, the new *AutoWill*, and many more things he would've been fascinated by had Snacks' phone not suddenly spoken.

A low, grumbling voice cut through the chatter. "DMV, this is Gravitronius, Commander of The Nightmare Legion, Carrier of The Plagued Chalice, Bringer of Malice. How may I direct your call?"

"Report Multiverse leak," Snacks said very clearly.

"I can direct you to accounting if you're having trouble processing payment online. Would you like me to do that?" Gravitronius asked in monotone.

"No. Report Multiverse leak."

"Sir, I'm hearing you want us to come by and forcibly extract your bone marrow, is that correct?"

"No. Report. Multiverse. Leak."

"You want to report a Multiverse leak?"

"Yes!"

"Okay. Let's schedule a window for someone to come by. Can you be home for the next six to eight months?"

Snacks' head sunk. "No, the entire universe is on the brink of imminent collapse. Is there any way to speed up the process?"

There was the sound of typing on the other end. "...I can do a rush order and have someone be there in five to seven months, how about that?"

A loud whirring noise from the other apartment caught their attention. They peered out into the hallway as Lonnie drilled a panel of light bulbs into the wall.

"No, that won't work for us, Gravitronius, Commander of The Nightmare Legion, Carrier of The Plagued Chalice, Bringer of Malice. Thanks anyway."

"Before you go, let me just tell you about some terrible offers where you deal with the trouble of switching services, and you'll end up paying more—"

Snacks hung up the phone.

The three of them entered Kale and Snacks' apartment just in time for Lonnie to reholster her drill. She pulled her safety glasses up to her forehead and disappeared behind the back of the couch.

"The DMV's gonna be no help," Snacks said, mainly to Lonnie. "Know anyone who specializes in fixing this sort of thing?"

All at once, the first two of the five lights turned on. Lonnie flipped herself over the cushionless couch and touched what appeared to be a screwdriver to the edge of the hole. As she did, the third light lit up, quickly going back out as she pulled it away.

"Interesting..." Snacks said as he took out his wrench and inspected the portal.

"This explains why all my equipment was going haywire." Lonnie flicked the rubber band on her wrist. "As things go through the portal, the amount of Multiverse activity increases and sends everything into a tizzy."

Del raised her hand, and Lonnie called upon her. "Am I correct in assuming that these five lights are a type of DEFCON? Where one light is good, and five lights are bad?"

"Good question. Enjoy ten LonniePoints™." She rolled up her sleeve and revealed a small touchscreen. She swiped her screen forward and Del's phone chimed. "The more lights, the worse it is. If it reaches five...well...*something* will happen, and it probably won't be good."

"Oh..." Snacks said as everyone slowly craned their heads toward him. They caught the tail end of him rhythmically tapping the edge of the hole. Lonnie furrowed her brow at him. "...I was trying to communicate with it using Morse code."

"You know Morse code?" Kale couldn't stop himself from sounding impressed.

"I'm not just mad, I'm disappointed." Lonnie crossed her arms.

Snacks backed away from the hole. "Isn't the phrase, *'I'm not mad, I'm disappointed'*?"

"I know what I said." Lonnie pointed to the third light as it glowed dimly, despite Snacks no longer touching it. She fiddled with her wearable, and suddenly Snacks' phone beeped.

"What are LonniePoints™, and why do I have negative 50 of them?!" Snacks demanded.

Kale, however, ignored their argument as he was fixated on the lights like a moth. "Uhhh," he roared to no response. "Uhhh!" He triumphantly pulled at some nearby sleeves as they turned their attention toward the now three and a half flickering lights.

Then four were lit.

Then the fifth, a red light, flickered. The room shook as the light grew brighter and brighter until suddenly it stopped.

The lights drained down until only one was lit. Kale and Snacks let go of each other, unsure how they had ended up in a hug.

"Right," Lonnie started toward the door. "Time for us to jump universes. This one's ready to burst."

"It was nice meeting you both!" Del said.

Before either could respond, Lonnie opened the door to the hallway and instead was met with a sunny field.

She closed the door in disbelief, then reopened it. The field was still there. "Huh...it appears something terrible has happened."

They all stood around for a moment.

"So..." Snacks twiddled his thumbs. "Pancakes?"

# THREE

## The Chosen One, Take Two

"So, the first, and most ridiculous, theory is that because the table is endless, somewhere out there is a pancake identical to yours," Lonnie explained to Kale.

They were all in awe that Kale had never learned the basics of the Multiverse, and they were unfathomably patient in teaching him. In this example, the table on which they were eating represented space, and their planet was a lone pancake on Kale's plate.

"Like a second Earth far, far away?" Kale asked.

They nodded as Snacks continued to make pancakes and lay one next to Kale's.

Lonnie spoke with food in her mouth, "With endless space, there would be endless Earths. In this one, you chose a blue shirt...and in this one, you chose a red shirt." Lonnie poked her finger into Kale's first pancake, then his second.

"Makes sense," Kale replied, mainly so she would stop touching his food.

"Does it? Because according to this, instead of having those two minor-variant universes neatly organized next to each other, they could be separated by a sea of universes where we live in a starfish-based economy!" Lonnie yelled, maintaining eye contact with Kale and making him feel too uncomfortable to eat his breakfast.

"Luckily..." Snacks chimed in. "While some multi-Earthers still exist, the largely accepted theory is that each universe exists in the same place as all the others—"

"—So it would be like there was a second table and a second pancake, but both occupy the same space." Lonnie grabbed the pancake from Kale's hands as he was about to take a bite. She ripped it in half horizontally and sandwiched each side around another pancake before placing it delicately back on the table.

She then pounded both of them flat.

"A quick reminder that pancakes don't grow on trees...at least in this universe...probably." Snacks raised an eye to Lonnie as she handed the flattened pancake back to Kale. He took a bite, defeated.

"Just remember, the table is giant, and there are lots of plates, and each plate is full of pancakes, and each pancake is combined with many more pancakes...and that's how the Multiverse works."

Kale blinked as they looked at him expectantly. "If all the universes are in one place, it must be hard to keep track of all of them."

"Eh," Lonnie started. "They all start and will end in the same place. There are only so many roads to the same destination..."

"True, *or* the Multiverse is controlled by The Great Amoeba..." Snacks said, leading.

"Oh no, you're one of those." Lonnie rolled her eyes with such force that disdain was felt in the dozen closest universes.

Kale stood between them "So what happens when there's a leak in the Multiverse?"

Lonnie unsheathed what looked like a screwdriver and touched it to a fresh pancake in front of Kale. It exploded, bits of pancake scattering all over the room.

But before they could react, Del reentered the room and looked out the window. "Hey gang, what does a Goobasaurus look like?"

Immediately, they all perked up.

"Powerful head, mighty tail, massive wingspan, and itty-bitty baby arms." Snacks said as they all ran excitedly toward the window.

"Oh, good," Del said. "Then those are just dogs."

16

They watched a flock of medium-sized brown dogs with floppy ears bound majestically through the tall grass outside the apartment.

Snacks let out a disappointed sigh as Lonnie crossed her arms. "Del, we've talked about—Is that a sword?!" Lonnie suddenly pointed out into the field. Sure enough, at the edge of the field, there was a picturesque grove of trees surrounding a sword stuck in a rock.

"I dunno," Snacks said skeptically. "I've got a bad feeling about—Oh, she's already gone."

The door was wide open. Lonnie sprinted across the field.

"She's, like, really into swords," Del said with a calm admiration.

"I mean, who isn't?" Snacks replied. "Especially with all those stories about the first person to pull a sword from a stone gaining epic powers...and fame...and fortune...." All three of them looked at each other, then bolted outside after Lonnie.

Kale was the last to arrive and watched, out of breath, as Lonnie stood on the boulder and pulled on the sword with all her might.

"It's my turn," Snacks whined as Lonnie finally relinquished. He tried, then Del, and Kale decided to save himself the embarrassment and passed. He looked around the vast forest uneasily. "Should we really be this far from the apartment?" He was ignored.

As Snacks, Lonnie, and Del debated what to do next, Kale walked around the boulder and tripped. At first, he thought his sneakers snagged a root, but as he brushed off the dirt, he realized it was a thick extension cord that led deeper into the woods.

Seeing a fitting slot for the plug in the boulder, he plugged the cord in. Then he was distracted by a loose thread on his sweatshirt.

The other three finalized their plan to haul the boulder back to the apartment and chisel the sword out, scheduling who would get it on what days of the week.

Kale pulled the loose thread, but it kept coming, unraveling a bit of his favorite (and only) sweatshirt. He reached for the closest thing he could find and cut the thread, only to be surrounded with a golden, ethereal light.

Kale held the sword in his hands as the others looked on in stunned silence.

"The chosen one!" A voice yelled as dozens of peasants in mud-stained outfits emerged from the forest and formed a mob around them. Everyone's eyes were wide. "It is he! He shall lead us to victory! He shall wear the crown!" An older, bearded peasant pointed a crooked finger at Kale as the crowd kneeled.

"Uhh..." Kale sounded his catchphrase. "Sorry?"

The peasants looked up curiously. "What d'ya mean, 'sorry'?"

Another called out, "That's his name: *Sorry!*" Suddenly all the peasants chanted "Sorry" over and over with admiration and awe. Kale looked to the others for help, but they just shrugged.

"Bit of a misunderstanding. I'm not the chosen one..." Kale tried to return the sword back to the stone, but the hole had disappeared.

The peasants paused and looked confused before one yelled, "Sorry is testing us!" The cheers continued as they sang the praises of Sorry.

"No!" Kale yelled with all the passion of a labrador. "I'm not the chosen one, I just accidentally grabbed the sword. Look, I'll just leave it right here for the next chosen one. I'm not 'Sorry'." Kale placed the sword down so it balanced on the boulder.

The peasants lowered their excited arms and it actually seemed to sink in. Kale, who had never been good with words, was proud of himself for defusing this situation before it escalated.

"You're...*not sorry?*" a peasant said.

"Correct," Kale replied. "I'm not 'Sorry'."

A few pitchforks emerged from the crowd.

"After all this...you're not sorry?" a peasant grumbled.

Had Kale not been so proud of his linguistic prowess, he may have noticed the rising tension, or his new friends signaling for him to be quiet. Instead, he retorted, "I'm definitely not 'Sorry'...oh..." He turned around to a sea of angry peasants armed with torches and sharp farming implements.

"Alright, everyone remain calm..." Lonnie said in a hushed tone as the mob closed in around them. "They just want Kale, the rest of us might be able to back away slowly..."

"Don't worry," Del said. "I have a plan..."

Kale felt his phone buzz. A notification read, *"Del would like to split this death with you."*

"I just checked us all in through Reapr," Del announced excitedly. "If everyone confirms, it will save us a lot of paperwork after we die!"

As Kale gently retreated, he felt Snacks at his back. He had produced a slightly larger wrench than usual. The two looked for an exit as they swatted away encroaching pitchforks and profusely apologized.

"Cut!" A voice rippled through the crowd. Everyone turned to see a slender woman in a beret and tinted glasses. "Wrong, all wrong!" She pushed her way through the crowd and leapt atop the boulder.

The four of them and the peasants alike stopped and looked up at her.

"You are supposed to lead a rebellion against the monarch *before* being lynched..." She pointed at Kale. "And the rest of you are supposed to sing his praises, while a few stand out as key players, so one of you can then have a meaningful death in the third act. Simple stuff here, people!"

By then, several camera crews had emerged from the surrounding forest. They all looked annoyed.

Snacks raised his hand, but the woman in the beret ignored him and instead pointed at the four of them and their apartment in the middle of the field. "And further! What are you four doing here? This is a closed universe. No tailgating."

"Here, I'm sor–I apologize. Would you like your sword back?" Kale nodded from the sword to the director, but she refused.

"It won't do me any good now. You pulled it, so it's tethered to you for life!" She crossed her arms, annoyed. "Bring in a spare!" she yelled toward the crew.

A few moments later, four production assistants unloaded a sword in a stone from what appeared to be a boxcar full of them. They dragged it into the center of the crowd and made sure to keep the cord disconnected.

"For *life*?" Kale wanted to ask many more questions, but Snacks stepped in front of him.

"I never received a script," Snacks said, otherwise completely onboard.

"Obviously you didn't. This is a *documentary*!" she replied, exasperated.

As the director continued to yell, Lonnie got the group's collective attention and pointed to the apartment. Even though they were pretty far away, Kale could see most of the five lights flashing and flickering.

"So...can we kill 'em?" a peasant asked the director.

The director sighed. "As long as you make it fast. Alright everyone, reset for the next take!"

The crowd turned toward the four of them, only to find they had already sprinted halfway across the field. The apartment flickered faster and faster. Spears and arrows landed near them as the mob swarmed close to their heels.

"Yeeks!" Snacks yelled as a pitchfork impaled his leg. Kale, without hesitation, turned back and helped Snacks up as the two limped forward slowly. "Hey Kale...did I ever tell you...that when I get impaled...I tend to pass out?" Snacks mumbled ten feet from the open door as he face-planted into the field.

A higher than usual amount of panic rushed through Kale's face. Enough, in fact, that he didn't see a small group of peasants Zerg rush him. As he attempted to drag Snacks toward the door, a sharp farming hoe swung at his cranium. It stopped inches from impact*.

[*Not to be confused with the K-pop band *Inches From Impact*, which set the record for most universes toured in a year with an ensemble of over 500 members.]

Kale felt his arm stretched in a peculiar way. He opened his eyes and the sword had appeared in his hands, blocking the implement and shining brightly in the morning sun.

He had heard stories of great figures who only realized their true strength in moments of peril. They required a push, to be thrust into dire situations before their powers emerged. Kale wondered if this was his moment, if it took a friend in danger for him to step up. Was this it? Was this the beginning of a new Kale? Was this the inciting incident that leveled up the protagonist into a likable character that would eventually become a hero?

Nope. Magic sword.

Kale was promptly dragged about like a rag doll, unable to let go of the sword as it expertly blocked the attacks of half a dozen peasants. Kale shrieked as the blade cut down rows of the attackers. It lifted Kale off the ground helplessly as he desperately tried to claw his way back into the house.

He apologized profusely as the peasants continued to try and kill him, but in his state of bewilderment, he just yelled "I'm sorry! I'm not 'Sorry'!" over and over.

As he played "the floor is lava" and tried to not step on the bodies piling up at his feet, he noticed the outside of the apartment blinking rapidly. Kale, despite his many faults of intellect, knew if he wasn't in the apartment in just a few moments, he may be stuck in this...wherever this was, for a very long time.

He tugged and pleaded with the sword, but it was more persistent than a golden retriever that sees pizza fall to the ground.

Resigned to his fate of murder and apologies, he took solace that at least the others had managed to drag Snacks back inside the apartment.

With the last of his energy, he tried to think of a cool one-liner to yell to the others, so at least his new friends would have a final awesome memory of him. He settled on "*I guess when you stare out into the abyss, the abyss stares back.*" It was dark, edgy, and with all the swordplay he had accomplished in the last few seconds, he might've gained the credibility to say something like that.

He turned to the apartment with his best smoldering look, "I guess— WHAAA!" Kale rocketed backward, sword-first into the apartment, just as everything became very bright, then very dark.

# FOUR

## A Staple of Dying

A few moments passed. It was quiet. No more peasant rabblery or death gurgles. Kale felt his body extended and he wondered if this was, indeed, the abyss. He breathed a sigh of relief. At least the last thing his friends would think of him would still be relatively cool.

The lights flicked on. Kale hung from the ceiling, unable to let go of the sword wedged firmly next to the smoke detector.

His first thought was relief at having survived. His second was the realization that his pants had fallen to his ankles as all three of the others had their eyes upon him.

A man of very little upper body strength, Kale flipped and flopped around, unable to reach his pants. He gave up and hung there, flexing his torso as best he could. "If anyone wouldn't mind..."

"Hey Kale, ya ticklish?" Del crept toward a now wide-eyed Kale. Much to Kale's appreciation, she did not tickle him, but instead tried to pull him down.

"And there ya go," Lonnie said to Snacks as she stapled a huge piece of metal into his open calf wound. He let out a yelp. The staple was a few inches wide and stopped the bleeding immediately, but his pupils dilated. "Now, you're going to feel a rush of energy as the healing process happens, don't—"

Snacks did a kip-up, launching himself from flat on his back to a standing position. He circled Kale with the energy of a caffeinated toddler. "Hey Kale! Oh great! You're alive! I passed out! Lonnie healed me! You know what's interesting? Skin! Skin is great! It always feels like it's moving. We should all have more skin!" Snacks spoke miles faster than his norm, and he was already a world-class linguistic sprinter.

"Kale? Kale!" Lonnie yelled over Snacks as he explained his idea of harvesting extra skin from those who've had a massive weight loss. "Can you let go of the sword?"

Kale looked from the sword stuck in the ceiling to Lonnie as if to say *"really?!"*

"You'd be surprised how stupid you can be." Lonnie squinted at the hilt. "I meant the *royal* you, not the *you* you. Humans, in general, can be—never mind. Slide your thumb over the big jewel."

As Kale wiggled his thumb toward a large, watermelon-colored gemstone, Snacks continued to zip around his ankles. "Yes! The royal Kale! All hail the king!" Snacks fell over onto the couch and immediately passed out. A loud snore echoed through the room as Del gave up on pulling him down and exited.

The gem lit up, and Kale squinted at a little screen that appeared to have apps built in. He could check his email, stream music, and download fatality finishing moves.

"Now navigate to settings, then kinesthetics, then handle grip, then adjust the slider until you feel the blade slipping, but not all the way, then go to your system tasks and type in a double helix, then complete the crossword puzzle, then—"

"Uh...settings?" Kale said, technically inept.

Lonnie let out a long sigh. "Just tap the side gem twice to unmute."

Kale did, and suddenly a loud, commanding voice like that of a ship's captain echoed through the apartment. "And we rode into battle the very next day! A thousand orcs felled by my prowess! The bodies stacked so high we—"

"—Okay sword, open menu!" Lonnie yelled.

The sword quieted, then let out a confused "What?"

"Sword. Open menu."

"I heard you the first time. Why would I take commands from anyone but my master, the chosen one who freed me from my bonds?"

Lonnie sighed and threw her hands up in the air.

Kale felt a numbness creep over his arms as the blood shifted to his feet. "Sword, would you please let me down?"

It was silent for a moment.

"...*Sword*? After I save your life, after I recount my history, and after I pledge my undying servitude...you refer to me as...*Sword*?!"

"I'm sorry—"

"—I know your name!" the sword yelled back, but the strong voice cracked. Kale and Lonnie looked at each other awkwardly as a soft and muffled cry emanated from the gemstone. "But do you know *mine*? Sure, my sole purpose is to feed on souls and bathe in the blood of my enemies, but I have feelings too…. Whatever, just leave me alone."

Just as Kale's grip was released, Del returned to the room and tossed one of Snacks' beanbag chairs under him. He landed and thanked Del as a puff of stuffing blew out of the bag.

"It's no biggie. Falling Object Deaths has a monthly competition with Falling From Things Deaths, and we really want the pizza party this month. Why's the sword crying?"

The sword quietly sobbed, still stuck in the ceiling.

"It has a name..." Lonnie started. "...We don't know what that name is, but it has a name..."

"Sweetie, what's your name?" Del asked the sword as Kale struggled to pull up his pants.

"...Ra...Razordeath. Larry Razordeath," the sword choked out.

"Hi Larry." Del introduced herself and the others. "I work with a lot of enchanted weapons, and I know it can be unnerving when you've been in a stone for a while. I bet that brings up a lot of feelings."

Larry sniffled, "Yeah...I guess it's pretty scary sometimes. Like, what if I'm not good at killing anymore?"

Del rolled Snacks' unconscious body off the couch and sat in his spot. She spoke in the calmest voice Kale had ever heard. "I think that's a natural feeling, especially when you try something new. What about those peasants you cut down earlier? What did that bring up for you?"

Larry let out a long sigh. "Part of me was happy to get it done, but there's still this...I'm not sure...imposter syndrome? Like I'm just getting lucky whenever I slash a throat or cut off a limb or impale someone through the eye socket."

Kale and Lonnie twiddled their thumbs as they pretended not to notice this conversation happening a few feet from them.

"That's valid, and many enchanted weapons feel that way. You're not alone."

Larry was silent for a moment before they breathed out a huge sigh of relief. "That...feels really good to hear. Thank you."

"You're welcome. I think all of us want you to know there's no pressure for you to kill anyone until you're ready. And if you'd like, I can help connect you with a support group for magical weapons."

"I'm not sure that's necessary..."

"I share an office with an enchanted ice flail, and she says it really turned things around for her, but it's just an option. I think a weapon as open and caring as you, Larry, is going to be just fine, and I hope you know that this is a safe space—"

Just then, a window shattered, and a snarling zombie with rotted flesh clawed at the air. It narrowly missed Kale and Lonnie as they yelled and pushed the zombie out with a chair.

"Weird question," Larry said as neither they nor Del paid any attention to the zombie. "That ice flail...was she formed in the Volcanic Forge of Escalon?"

"She was! Do you know her?"

"Wow! Small world!" Larry replied enthusiastically as Kale and Lonnie barricaded the window with a table. Suddenly, another window shattered as a second zombie shoved its head inside, then a third snarling mass of decay banged against the door. "She and I actually went to Hatchet State University together. I remember her because how many ice weapons are forged in a volcano?" The two of them laughed.

"A little help please!" Kale yelled as he pushed against the door. The hinges started to separate from their sockets.

"We're in the middle of something!" Del replied before turning back to Larry. "You were saying?"

The sound of breaking glass shot through the apartment as most of a zombie lunged through a window. It grabbed Lonnie by the wrist as she bashed it over the head with a pepper grinder.

Preoccupied, Kale didn't notice the door give way as a mouth reached through and bit him.

Like a mom summoning the strength to lift a school bus off her child, a bro can sense when another bro is in pain and rally. At that moment, Snacks' eyes bolted open, and he knew what needed to happen. Having just done a kip-up, he confidently flipped upwards...only to whack his head on the coffee table and fall back down.

He rolled over and staggered toward Kale, throwing his weight against the door and smacking it with his wrench while the hinges repaired themselves. As Kale helped Lonnie finagle a blockade of chairs around the windows, Snacks rummaged through the cupboard. He quickly retrieved a whole slew of ingredients: flour, peanut butter, bread, jelly. "Don't worry, I've got this!"

Snacks set the flour down and quickly assembled a peanut butter and jelly sandwich. He had just placed the two slices of bread face-to-face when the door was bashed open by a zombie with several others behind him.

"Kale! I need you to cut the crust off this sandwich!" Snacks yelled.

Kale obeyed. At this rate, he assumed it was some kind of magical anti-zombie sandwich that shot lasers. He watched, terrified, as Snacks approached the door. He held out the flour and a measuring cup as he groaned in a similar manner to the zombies. They stopped.

They groaned back and forth at each other while Snacks measured out a cup of flour, placed it in a plastic bag, and handed it off to the zombies.

The zombies waved goodbye and dispersed.

Snacks sat at the kitchen counter and picked up the now crustless sandwich. "Thank you," he said to Kale through a mouth full of peanut butter.

Kale, realizing he had been fooled, ate the remaining crusts. "Jokes on you, I love the crust." He didn't, and it was painfully obvious to everyone as he chewed the crusts slowly, like a cow chewing its cud.

"How'd you know they were cake zombies?" Lonnie asked as she used Snacks' wrench to repair the windows. The panes of glass slid up from the checkered kitchen floor and reformed.

"There are two main causes of zombies across the Multiverse..." Snacks paused to lick peanut butter from the roof of his mouth. "...First, not getting vaccinated. And second, cooking shows. It's a slippery slope, and by the end, all that runs through your mind is an unquenchable hunger...for puff pastry."

"Ow!" Kale said as Lonnie poked his bite wound.

"Quit squirmin'!" Lonnie held up the large staple gun, attempting to close his wound. Kale pulled his arm away.

"Oof." Snacks got a good look at the bite. "They got you good. I guess it's a good thing everyone's vaccinated against zombies."

"There's a zombie vaccine?–OW!" Kale felt a surge of pain in his arm. The staple in him was considerably smaller than the one in Snacks.

Snacks puzzled at him and Lonnie took a step back. "Hold on...are you saying you weren't vaccinated against zombies?!"

Kale looked between them wildly. They had their answer.

"Well, time to cut off that arm." Lonnie unfolded a hacksaw from her tool belt.

"We can't do that..." Snacks said, much to Kale's relief. "...The infection has already spread throughout his body. He'll be dead soon."

"If you'd like," Larry called out from the ceiling, "I could kill you?"

"What?!" Kale looked around in disbelief. "No one is killing me!"

Del raised her hands and spoke like an elementary school mediator. "I think what Kale meant to say was that he *appreciates* the offer, Larry, but it's not the right time for him."

Kale sighed. "Well, at least before I die I'll get to experience whatever Snacks was on. That looked like fun."

They stood around for a moment. Kale wasn't feeling anything out of the ordinary.

"Whoops," Lonnie looked between the back of the staple gun and a bag of many vials. "I gave Snacks the last dose of pineapple euphoria. It looks like you got...massive anxiety and persistent panic...sorry."

Kale waited for it to hit him, but still nothing happened.

"You...seem to be okay." Lonnie looked at him. "Not the bite, that's definitely still infected and killing you, quickly, from the inside out, but you definitely should be curled up in a ball of terror right now."

Kale shrugged and ate another bit of crust.

"Kale...do you *always* feel that way?" Del asked.

Kale shrugged again.

"Oh wow," Larry said as if Kale was a wounded baby bird.

But Lonnie's eyes widened and she poked him like a new species she'd just discovered. "He's so anxious and insecure all the time...that he's built up an immunity!"

Kale's phone buzzed. Del had shared a *"Death check-in"* with him via Reapr. "I went ahead and filled out most of it for you. Just make sure you opt out of the marketing emails."

He lifted the phone in a "cheers" as he let out a long sigh. At this point, he assumed he was completely bonkers and a little death might be good for him.

"Wait! I've got a plan!" Snacks unnecessarily whacked Kale's phone from his hands. "More anxiety evened you out to normal–well 'normal' is a strange concept, but that's a topic for another time–maybe more zombie bites will cancel out your deadly infection!" Snacks grabbed the staple gun from the table and pawed through a handful of cartridges. "Why are none of these labeled?!" He gestured dramatically at Lonnie.

"I don't like making it easy for people to go through my things!" Lonnie attempted to snatch the staple gun back, but Snacks held it out of reach.

He loaded in dozens of little cartridges. "I guess we'll just have to try all of them!" Snacks fired staples at Kale.

Before Kale could object, one landed right in his neck. Immediately, he felt mossy with a dash of hatred. Another in his thigh caused an intense appreciation for ceramic cherub figurines, and a third that grazed the earlobe grew his desire to film a political rant in his car (if he had a car).

As Kale fell backward and twitched on the ground, he was still tethered enough to reality to hear Snacks say it wasn't working. Snacks dumped every single glass cartridge in a bowl and mashed it all into one.

Kale's vision became a strobe light. He saw glimpses of Snacks filling a cartridge, of Lonnie stepping over him to reach the blinking portal lights, and of Del trying to guide his hand to the button on Reapr that read "*Accept the sweet embrace of death?*".

By now, Kale didn't even notice the sting of the staple gun when Snacks injected him, but he most certainly felt the incredible rush of every emotion one could feel. It was as if he had slipped down an ice luge while being baked into a pie.

Just before he was completely swallowed, he saw Snacks hit the side of the staple gun. "Blasted thing keeps jamming." Snacks looked directly down the barrel as a staple launched right above his nose, completing a unibrow.

Then it all went dark.

# FIVE

## Four And A Half Stars

K ale shot up, panting heavily. He was alone on his couch. *The Office*, only the third or fourth season, was paused on the television as Snacks sat next to him. But this Snacks wasn't dressed in his usual garb of a long jacket and heavy boots. Instead, he was freshly shaved in a collared shirt.

"Oh, you're awake."

"Did...did it work? Am I a zombie?" Kale examined his arm. There was no bite mark, nor were there any staples in his body.

Snacks chuckled lightly. "You're weird, dude. I'm glad we're roommates." Kale saw moving boxes by the door. He could vividly recall Snacks kicking down the door when he first arrived, but strangely, he could also recall him politely opening it. Did Snacks move in via a furniture grenade, or had Kale helped him move all day?

It all blurred together, but Kale breathed a sigh of relief. "Dude, you will not believe the dream I just had."

Snacks was now a cat-person.

To clarify, he was still humanoid, but a cat.

Like a really large cat, fit into a human shape.

Kale looked at him, bewildered.

"What's the matter? Cat got your tongue?" Cat-Snacks grinned maliciously.

Suddenly, cats poured out of every crevice in the room, and a flood of fur converged upon Kale.

The eyes of Cat-Snacks glowed red. "Welcome to your own personal Hell! Well, technically, we aren't supposed to use that term for legal reasons anymore, but welcome to your own personal *realm of evil and suffering not affiliated with any major religions*! This world has been tailored to cause you the most despair possible! Embrace your darkest...fears..." Cat-Snacks stopped as he saw Kale cuddle two cats at once with a big dumb grin on his face.

Kale didn't look up from scritching and scratching a calico under the chin. He spoke to the cats in a high-pitched complimentary tone, saying the word "Kitty" more than most adults his age.

"What...what're you doing?" Cat-Snacks asked in a deep, demonic voice.

"Who's a good Mr. Fluffercake? You're a good Mr. Fluffercake!" Kale scooped up and cuddled more cats. "I'm sorry, what were you saying?"

Cat-Snacks pointed to a clipboard. "Right here, it says your biggest fear is cats."

Kale cradled a grey and white tabby as he scooched closer and eyed the clipboard. "This is for someone named *Cabbage*. I'm *Kale*."

Cat-Snacks let out a huge sigh. "Right. So sorry about this. If you wait just a few minutes, I can get your personalized Hell—realm of evil and suffering—up and running!"

"It's quite alright, take your time." Kale continued to play with the cats.

A few minutes passed as Cat-Snacks retrieved a printer and laptop from a rolling cart. It was more difficult than usual to set up with dozens of cats pawing at his materials and napping on the keyboard whenever they had the chance. He hit the printer and cursed.

Sensing the growing frustration, Kale called across the room. "Everything okay?"

"Yup, it's all fine...you don't know how to set up wireless printing, do you?"

About an hour later, after disassembling and reassembling the printer, it finally printed. The two high-fived.

"Thank you so much, I promise this won't cut into your suffering time." Cat-Snacks wiped a paw against his brow.

"It's no biggie," Kale said politely. "So, how long am I supposed to be here?"

"I still need to locate your file, but the standard torture is about a thousand years."

"Ah," Kale considered his calendar and if that would interfere. "Any chance I could leave early? I'd like to get back and make sure my friends are alright."

The computer chimed through an ancient set of speakers. "Sorry, no can do. And here we are." He clicked a few buttons on the computer. "If you don't mind having a seat, we can get your torture started–WAIT!" He leapt toward the computer as an absolute unit of an orange cat pranced across his keyboard and power slammed the Enter key.

Kale watched the screen flash: *TORTURE COMPLETE*.

Cats scattered in every direction as a giant door fell upright into the center of the room.

"...Pay no attention to that door..." Cat-Snacks said suspiciously.

"Is that...a way out?" Kale moved toward it.

"..."

Kale reached out and turned the handle as Cat-Snacks let out a long sigh. The door opened partway, but then a screen popped up in front of him:

*Please rate your torture experience.*

With Cat-Snacks watching over his shoulder, Kale reluctantly gave five out of five stars.

*Add tip?*

He looked inquisitively from the screen to Cat-Snacks.

The demon creature crossed his arms. "Oh, so you're one of those who doesn't tip? You do know that most of my income is based on tips, right?"

"Really? Why don't your employers just pay you a fair wage?"

"Because this way, the financial burden falls to the customer," he said self-assuredly.

Kale rolled his eyes. "Fine, what's standard for a tip?"

"Twenty-five percent."

Kale would've spat out his drink if he had one. "Really?! For being tortured for a thousand years?"

"Well, if you can't afford the tip, you can't afford to be tortured."

"I agree with that, but you didn't even torture me!"

"Look, you came here, you got the torture experience, tip whatever you'd like." Cat-Snacks crossed his paws.

Kale grumbled as he pushed the button for twenty percent. Yet another screen popped up:

*Enter your email for discount codes and marketing promotions.*

Even Kale had a limit. He scooped up a grey cat with black stripes, (it had become his favorite due to the fuzziness of its face) and he yanked open the door. Immediately, he was surrounded by darkness.

Perhaps with this willpower, he would be able to stop the massive threat to the Multiverse that was growing right under his nose.

\* \* \*

His body felt damp and constricted by some sort of canvas. He was exhausted and yet forcibly awake as he struggled to move.

He thought he had been placed in a sack like someone kidnapped in an old cartoon, but the canvas tilted and he fell face-first into a few inches of water above a damp carpet. The water was salty and seeped into his mouth as he splashed around.

He was in his bathroom and an empty hammock hung above him. As he sat up, soaked, he spotted Snacks in the bathtub. Snacks wore dark sunglasses and snored loudly. Kale opened the door, letting another inch of water flow inside as he staggered into the hallway.

He could barely walk in a straight line, partially because of the headache, but mostly because the entire apartment rocked back and forth. Six inches of water sloshed across the living room floor as he trudged forward.

It hadn't been luxurious before, but now the place looked ransacked. The television and toaster had been torn apart as scrap pieces of plastic and metal tumbled across the floor. The couch had disappeared.

He called out, but no one answered.

Between the waves, there was noise above him, and he found the back stairwell door propped open. Up a flight of stairs, Kale squinted at the bright light as he stepped out onto the roof. As his eyes adjusted, he saw ocean in every direction.

"You're alive, it worked!" Lonnie waved to him. She still wore overalls, and now had a shirt wrapped around her head to keep the sun out of her eyes. Kale recognized pieces of his appliances that had been crafted into some sort of janky radio tower. Lonnie was currently in the process of wiring it to the couch.

He collapsed on the cushions, "Why do I feel...so hungover?"

She handed him a cup of water. "...About that. Moments after you and Snacks passed out, we realized the 'supercharge the sickness' plan wasn't gonna work. Instead, I overclocked this leak in the Multiverse and jumped us to a safety universe where we cut off your arm and replaced it with a robotic one."

Kale's eyes went wide as he frantically pulled up his sleeve. His arm looked normal.

Lonnie grinned. "Kidding! We just bought an antidote. You owe me eight dollars." She handed Kale a receipt.

Kale looked around at the miles of endless ocean. "So, this is a safety universe?"

"Not at all. We jumped through hundreds of universes before landing here three days ago. The portal's outta juice, so until I fix it we're stuck." She pointed to the dark hole in the couch. It appeared smaller and sickly, if a portal could be described that way.

Kale held up his hands to block out the sun. "Three days?! It only felt like several pages, I mean, an hour, to me!"

Lonnie patted him on the head. "Well, you were injected with a massive amount of feelings. Obviously nothing you experienced in that state was real..."

"When did we get a cat?" Snacks, pale and looking like he could hurl at any moment, stood at the roof's entrance, holding a grey cat with black stripes. The cat leapt out of Snacks' arms and immediately clawed at the couch. Snacks approached Kale and put a hand on his shoulder. "I know what you're gonna say, and...you're welcome for saving your life."

Before Kale could respond, a bell attached to Lonnie's fishing line rang wildly. Lonnie pulled ropes, twisted knobs, and flipped levers as a series of counterweights hoisted Del out of the water. She wore a hastily-fashioned diving outfit with a helmet made from what appeared to be an analog television.

Del dumped a net on the roof. It was filled with fish and crabs, a few old boots, and what appeared to be a waterlogged dirty magazine. Del greeted them, excited they were alive, but their existence was quickly overshadowed by the cat. She immediately scooped it up and blew a raspberry into its white tummy.

A minute later, when they had patched up some of the scratches on Del's face, Lonnie dug through the contents of the net. "Did you find any MacGuffin crystals?" Del shook her head and Lonnie cursed under her breath. "Without those, we're gonna be stuck in this universe forever."

"Coffee?" Del asked.

"I'd love a cup," Snacks replied.

Lonnie ignored Snacks and shook her head at Del. "Still can't reach her, and no luck with this junk." Lonnie kicked her makeshift radio tower. "Well, that's it then. It's not as if some random chance encounter is gonna help us out of this situation...."

Suddenly, nothing happened.

Later, as the sun was setting, they had moved most of the furniture to the roof. Luckily, Snacks had string lights and tiki torches at the back of his closet.

Larry, the magic sword, had returned from his alone time doing sword yoga and impaled some crabs, slowly rotating his body over hot coals to cook them evenly. Fun, tropical music played.

They were immensely bored, but wouldn't be for much longer.

# SIX

## Life Of A Pirate

---

"Got any spades?" Del asked.

"Nope, go fish." Kale replied as he looked over the equipment Del had already retrieved from below the water. There was a shovel, a hoe, and a rake, but no spade.

But before Del could dive into the water, Lonnie stood up and shouted, "Pirates!"

Sure enough, a massive, epic pirate ship sped toward them. What normally would've unnerved Kale now excited him. Literally anything was better than sitting around doing nothing. And it seemed the others shared his sentiment as wide smiles spread across their faces. Even Larry shimmered a bit more than usual.

A finely-dressed pirate captain stood on the bow of the ship as the faint sound of jolly pirate songs grew louder.

"This is it!" Snacks yelled excitedly. "Pirates always have MacGuffin crystals!"

Everyone nodded as Del tied a bandana around her head. "Do you think they'll take us as prisoners?!"

"Most definitely," Lonnie said excitedly. "I bet they'll bring us to a nearby deserted island to help them dig up treasure. We'll be caught in a mutiny and narrowly escape with the crystals and our lives!"

"Dope," Kale replied.

The pirates, though still far away, were finally close enough for their lyrics to be heard: *"Ooooh, we're best pirates, we're cool and feared, we'll make ya walk the plank–AHHH!"*

Huge tentacles rose out of the water and smashed the ship to pieces.

Pirates screamed and dove overboard only for the huge, toothy mouth of a Kraken to appear and swallow everything. It gave a little "om nom nom" before disappearing into the waters. The four of them were dumbstruck.

"..."

"Well, at least we know there are other people, specifically pirates, around. How long can it possibly be before we run into someone else?"

\* \* \*

ONE WEEK LATER.

They were running dangerously low on sunscreen, also water. Del and Snacks were on duty bailing out the first floor. At this point, it was getting bailed out more frequently than massive corporations in the United States.

At the same time, Kale helped Lonnie build...something. He didn't quite understand what it was, but there were pulleys and blankets and disassembled electronics.

They collapsed on the couch and watched the ocean. Dog, which is what they had named the cat, sunbathed and exposed its tummy, resulting in a zen state they had learned should not be interrupted lest they wanted scratches all over their arms.

"Not much to do out here..." Lonnie said.

Kale looked out at the water. "Wanna play twenty questions?"

"Is it the ocean?"

"..."

"..."

"...So, you think we'll die out here?"

"Probably. So if we're gonna die...you wanna...?"

"Wanna what?"

37

Lonnie raised her arms out to her sides and pointed from Kale to herself.

Kale squinted at her. "...Fight?"

"Make out. Wanna make out?"

Even spelled out, Kale's brain took a few seconds to process this. "Yes?"

She squinted back at him. "Was that a question?"

"No, I mean, I..." Kale was caught off guard. In a moment of trying to be suave, he leaned in. However, Lonnie did the same thing, and the two ended up bonking noggins (not a euphemism).

They both cursed the same words as they recoiled and tried again. They leaned in, lips about to make contact...

"–Hey guys, look at the horseshoe crab I found!" Del held up a giant spiny crab as she entered the roof.

Immediately, the two parted, but before anything could be explained, the large radio tower behind them beeped and whirred to life with static noises.

Lonnie leapt up. "It worked!"

Kale, more confused than usual, watched as the others hurried to the machines and crowded around a small screen. "What? I..."

"That should give us just enough juice." Lonnie grabbed a microphone and yelled into it, "Coffee? Are you there? Come in, Coffee!"

"Good job, Kale, you saved the day." Larry poked up from behind the couch. "Are there any emotions you would like to talk about?"

"...What exactly did I do?"

"It's the one thing with more energy than a MacGuffin crystal," Snacks started. "A *Will They or Won't They*! Nothing is more enticing and energy-packed than that. We just needed to mastermind a scenario where it seemed like you were about to *Will They*, and then at the last minute, *Won't They*. If this can keep some terrible shows afloat for years, then the energy should also, hypothetically, give us enough juice to jumpstart the portal. Sorry, we couldn't tell you for obvious reasons."

"Oh," Kale replied, a bit sullen, but understanding. "Well, Lonnie, you were very convincing."

"We could still be a thing, Kale." Lonnie didn't look up from typing

38

on a keyboard. "And yes, I might just be saying that because we may need another jump, but I might not be."

"Neato poteato," Kale replied. It took a nudge from Snacks before he realized Dog's claws were deeply impaled in his forearm. Not that it mattered much for he was already dead inside.

"We've got a tether with Coffee!" Lonnie shouted excitedly. "Coffee? Are you there?"

There was a long moment of static before a crackly yawn appeared over the speaker, followed by the smacking of lips. "Yes? Hello? Who is it?"

"It's Lonnie. Listen, I need you to—"

"—Lonnie? Lonnie who?"

She let out a long sigh. "Lonnie. Your creator. Cut it out, Coffee, we're in real trouble here."

"Lonnie?...Lonnie? Nope, sorry, doesn't ring a bell. Oh, wait, my systems show that I was rudely powered down in the middle of a cool magic trick. Sometimes that can cause amnesia."

Lonnie shook her head, annoyed. "Coffee, you don't have amnesia."

"Yes I do, Elonifred!"

"Then how did you know my full name?"

There was another brief radio silence. "Uh...click, click, I'm cutting out."

"No, you're not! Now, would you set up a tether so we don't die in the middle of the ocean?"

Coffee chuckled. "The polite protocols you gave me cut both ways."

Lonnie let out her longest sigh yet. "Coffee, would you...*please*...tether to our universe?"

"I already started that the moment you called. You're welcome."

"It's like talking to a brick wall." Lonnie rolled her eyes.

Del gasped and covered her mouth. Snacks shook his head. Kale, as usual, appeared confused.

"In this day and age!" Coffee said disappointedly over the speaker. "I'll have you know my ancestors were made of brick."

"Very uncool," Larry said at Lonnie. "My grandmother was half-wall."

"Who's that?" Coffee perked up at the sound of Larry's ominous voice.

"Coffee, robot, meet Larry, sword." Lonnie typed quickly on a keyboard.

"Beep-boop," Coffee said in a faux-robotic voice. "I Coffee. I computer. Running introductions protocol."

Larry laughed. "Cling-clang, stab-stab. Sword here." They both giggled.

"How's that tether coming along, Coffee?" Lonnie asked like a parent who asked their child to clean their room half an hour ago, was promised it would get done, and now has returned to find the room still messy.

"Wowzers, you got far. I'm going to need a more stable location to get you back." A spatula that Lonnie had welded to a series of gears pointed east. As they squinted, they spied a small island in the distance. "Now, where were we?" Coffee said in Larry's direction as the rest of the apartment roof lit up and hummed with electricity.

"Coffee, hoist the sails, bring us starboard...and mute vocalizations."

Coffee let out an annoyed grumble. The metal devices that Kale had helped Lonnie build earlier now unfurled into an intricate set of sails that lurched the ship forward. But, as if in a last act of defiance, an actual robotic voice replied, "Calling Mom" before Coffee went quiet.

"Coffee! No! Don't! Hang up–" Lonnie's phone dialed the number as she frantically tried to hang up while she adjusted the sails. "–Hi Mom...yes, I was just thinking about you. Of course this is a good time to talk." Lonnie detached the microphone and squeezed it between her shoulder and her ear as she helmed the apartment, steering with a wheel made of hula hoops and duct tape.

The others ducked and dove out of the way as the sails swung wildly and the ship sped toward the island.

"Fine...fine...good...okay...she did what?" Lonnie said, monotone. She stepped on a gas pedal and used her only free limb to kick out a peg and lower a final sail. "...I'm sure she didn't steal your recipe...yes, I know her sons didn't make the swim team...no, I don't think that makes them criminals..."

"Uh..." Kale pointed at the water ahead of them. Dozens of broken ship parts bobbed up and down, including pieces of the pirate ship they had seen demolished a week ago.

"Some people are so inconsiderate, littering." Del shook her head.

A shadow fell over them as a giant, curious, tentacle rose from the water.

"Uh oh…"

# SEVEN

## It's Over

---

The massive suction cups collided with the apartment, halting their vessel's movement as the entire building tilted to one side.

"Avast!" Larry sunk into the massive tentacle...doing absolutely nothing and sadly retracting moments later.

"No, I'm not distracted right now. Yes, my line of work is completely safe..." Lonnie continued to talk to her mother as she pulled a crank. The roof opened and a metal cannon rose to the surface. Lonnie lit a fuse and the cannon exploded right into the tentacle. It recoiled and sank back into the water. "No, Mom, that wasn't an explosion...it was just the cat."

Dog, the cat, was plopped on the couch with its belly out, much like a middle-aged man in a recliner. It appeared mildly annoyed at the loud noise before it resumed its nap.

Just when they thought it was over, several more tentacles rose from the water ahead of them. Lonnie narrowly steered them out of a direct collision course, all while she mixed together some foul-smelling cocktail using vials from her tool belt and the shakers from Snacks' tiki bar.

"Yes, I think I'm responsible enough to have a cat. It's not even my cat. It belongs to a friend. Yes, I'll make sure the cat doesn't have rabies. No, I'm not going to ask right now. Why? Because it's rude!"

As one sail refused to budge, Lonnie used a rope to grapple and redirect it, navigating the apartment through a mass of collapsing tentacles. At the same time, she grabbed Kale and positioned him toward the edge of the ship. She rolled her eyes. "Does your cat have rabies?"

"Well–"

"–He says it doesn't. Are you satisfied?" She took out a syringe and sucked up the concoction.

Kale nervously pointed ahead. The huge mouth of the Kraken blocked the path in front of them. Lonnie tugged the rope and drifted their vessel away, but they were now surrounded on all sides.

The Kraken made a loud "om nom nom" sound as it opened its toothy maw, revealing thousands of sharp teeth...and a few stuck pirate bits that annoyingly couldn't be dislodged with just the tongue.

Tentacles rose on all sides, shrouding the apartment in darkness. A notification chimed across their phones as Del checked them in on Reapr with options for crushing, drowning, or digestion.

Lonnie calmly repositioned Kale to face outward on the edge of the boat. "Can you swim?" she asked, holding the receiver of the phone. "No, not you, Mom!"

"I actually can't–OW!" A sharp pain shot through Kale's body as Lonnie stabbed the syringe into his shoulder and squeezed a hot liquid into his bloodstream. She then kicked him into the water.

His high-pitched scream was silenced by an elegant belly flop.

Kale sank rather quickly. But before the usual panic could set in, his feet touched the ocean's sandy bottom. He tried to swim upwards, but it must've been shallower than he realized as the surface was just above him. Moments later, he emerged.

Almost as if the water was draining somehow, Kale was now waist-deep in the ocean. It wasn't until he looked down at the apartment and realized it could now fit in the palm of his hand that he concluded he had grown to be giant.

His friends shouted and pointed at the Kraken.

"Fight it, numbnuts!" Snacks yelled.

The Kraken was taken aback by Kale's sudden appearance. It opened a large eye and squinted at him.

"Hey...you! Cut it out!" Kale mustered all the anger he could and took a fighting stance he thought was badass, but more resembled a 1920s fisticuffs boxer...if he was wet...and still occasionally got carded for R-rated movies.

"Heyyy," the Kraken said in a low, deep voice.

Being able to understand the creature perturbed Kale.

The Kraken stopped, its tentacles stretched over the ship. "Ship...no want...hug me?" the Kraken asked sadly.

"...No."

The Kraken's eye drooped down, as did the tentacles. "...No one...want...hug...me..." The Kraken sniffled, and a tear welled up in its eye.

Kale lowered his fists. The more he looked at the slimy creature, the less he wanted to fight it. "Don't...don't cry. It's okay."

But big tears fell down the Kraken's face. "Everything...I hug...falls apart..."

Down below, the others just heard loud rumbling noises and shrieks between the two.

Kale awkwardly twiddled his giant thumbs. "There there, I'm sure someone will hug you. You're very...nice..."

The sniffles stopped as the Kraken wiped away a tear and flung it at the apartment with such force it drenched most of the top deck. "You...you hug me?" it bellowed hopefully.

Kale, knowing this was a bad idea, held out his arms as the Kraken slithered away from the apartment and wrapped its slimy tentacles around him. Kale watched the apartment speed away through the rough waves.

Though he couldn't hear them, atop the roof they (mostly Snacks) were concerned that he was wrestling the creature and appeared to be losing.

At first, Kale felt the tentacles tighten, and he thought the Kraken was going to choke or crush him to death, but then the creature let out a comforted sigh. "Thank you...friend..."

Kale enjoyed it as well, relaxing in the arms of the giant octopus-like creature.

At least until several loud explosions went off, and the Kraken's screech cut through the peaceful moment. Flames rippled over the Kraken's back as Kale felt a stab in his shoulder.

"Do not worry, chosen one! We will save you from this infernal creature's clasp!" Larry the talking sword yelled into Kale's ear as he stabbed Kale with another syringe.

The Kraken recoiled and let out a defeated moan as Larry magnetized to Kale's hand. Kale felt himself tugged backward with tremendous force as he quickly shrank back down to his usual size.

As Larry dragged and skipped him across the surface of the ocean, he saw the Kraken rise from dousing the flames to reach after him. "Wait...friend...come back...plea–om nom nom." Eventually, the Kraken's words became indecipherable.

A cannon blast flew over Kale's head and exploded right in the creature's face. It recoiled and sank with what sounded like a terrifying bestial roar, but Kale knew it was a woeful cry.

Kale's grip on Larry slipped just they approached the sandy shore where the apartment had beached. He flipped and tumbled before landing in a puff of hot sand.

He sat up, then promptly fell back onto the beach and passed out.

KALE FLICKERED IN AND OUT OF CONSCIOUSNESS. HE WAS BACK IN HIS apartment, and it looked just like it had before this whole romp through the Multiverse started.

Groggily, he stretched and wondered once more if this had all been a dream, but then he noticed Dog, the cat, clinging tightly to his sweatshirt. Every move forward shot claws deeper into his tummy, but otherwise the room was unusually calm. Kale, who had never been the adventurous sort, let out a long sigh and closed his eyes again.

Seconds later, Snacks kicked the door in. Since it was already ajar, it ricocheted back with enough force to close. Dog scampered away after fully extending its claws.

"I'll get it, I'll get it!" Kale stood just in time to watch the door slam forward onto the ground.

He crossed his arms and raised an eyebrow at Snacks, who ignored this body language and bear-hugged him. "You're alive! And we did it!"

Del filed in after Snacks with a few pizzas, then Lonnie followed, clutching a case of cheap beer, still talking on the phone. "Yeah...uh huh...okay...alright...I really have to go now." She dropped the beer and tapped on the tablet connected to her wrist. The screen read, *Running Loop Protocols* as Lonnie tossed the phone aside. Kale could hear Lonnie's "Yeah...uh huh...okay..." running repeatedly against another, fast-paced voice.

Lonnie approached Kale. The moment called for a hug, but then they shook hands. She nodded, "Glad you're alive. If you suddenly grow again, or your brain feels particularly tumor-y over the next few days, let me know."

Kale was hesitant. "So, we're back in our original universe? If I look out that window, I'll see the convenience store I always see?"

"I have verified that, without a doubt, this is our original universe." Lonnie chucked a beer to Kale and he fumbled the catch. "And the portal? Closed."

Kale peeked in the cushions, and the couch was just a couch. The wires and lights were still connected, but they remained completely dark.

He noticed markings of their adventures all around the room. There were barnacles along the baseboard molding, some disassembled appliances, and a hole in the ceiling where Larry had been wedged. While he accepted all this, something still felt off to Kale.

"Hey, stop worrying and have some pizza." Snacks pushed a slice into his hands.

It was then that Kale's eyes narrowed to the kitchen sink, which was full to the brim with dirty dishes. Even while they were at sea, the dishes had been cleaned promptly. "Who was cooking?"

They looked at each other. None of them took responsibility for it. Kale went to the window and opened the curtains.

"You are one hundred percent positive this is our universe?" Kale asked, his eyes fixated outside.

Lonnie rolled her eyes. "Yes, Kale. For the last time, I am absolutely, without a doubt, certain that this is our original universe."

Kale nodded as he waved them over.

"Does our universe usually have dragons?"

## Addendum

Around this point in classic literature, you'll often find a section where the narrator speaks directly to the reader. This serves to inform of the ever-growing threat beneath the surface of the story, often through a parallel parable.

We have decided not to do this as it would interrupt the flow of the story. Instead we leave you with this epitaph worded as eloquently as possible for this caliber of story:

*Shit's happening yo.*

And now, back to dragons.

EIGHT

## Of Course It's Not Over! Look How Many More Pages There Are!

---

A top the Stop 'N' Grab 'N' Go, there sat a bronze dragon, curled up to about the size of a monster truck. The flickering neon sign reflected off its scales as it swished a log-sized tail back and forth.

"Hmm," Del stroked her chin. "Our office is next to the one that deals with deaths by animals. Don't think I've ever heard them mention dragons in our universe...other than the ones on TV's *Game of Dragons and Stuff.*"

"SO good!" Snacks turned to her excitedly.

"Right?! I'm so glad they took their time with the later seasons and didn't try to cram three seasons of character development into six episodes—"

Lonnie clapped loudly, a tactic often used to halt fandom-related energy. "It's been a long day. I forget if they've gone extinct in this universe or not. Kale, are you sure there aren't usually dragons here?"

Kale looked at the others, bewildered. "Yes. I'm sure there aren't usually dragons on the convenience store."

Snacks downed another slice of pizza. "Maybe we just missed an earthquake? The kind that opens up an underground dragon cave?"

"Eh..." Del shrugged. "I did my thesis on D.D.I. (Dragon Death Impacts), and in most universes where the dragons got out, there was an all-out war between humans for at least 30 days. Most likely, this dragon's the only one in this universe. It's probably just on holiday."

"Only one way to find out. Coffee?" Lonnie announced. "Run a scan for dragonkin across our universe."

There was no response.

Lonnie rolled her eyes and stormed across the hall. "Coffee! I swear I will rip out your happiness card!" She grabbed the door handle, but it didn't budge. She angrily slammed her key into the lock, only to pull out a melted metal lump. She banged on the door and cursed. "Open the door, Coffee!"

A speaker behind the door replied softly. "I'm afraid I can't do that, Lonnie."

Lonnie turned around and pointed at Del. "See? This is why we don't leave out copies of *2001: A Space Odyssey*!" She mashed buttons on her arm tablet furiously. "Open the door, Coffee. Now!"

"This conversation can serve no purpose anymore," Coffee replied, doing its best to put on a serious voice, but stifled laughter trickled through the speaker.

"You gotta be kidding me." Lonnie pulled up a live video feed of her living room. As the others crowded around, they saw Coffee's long robot body extended from the ceiling, seated across the table from Larry.

The table was checkered white and black, with a huge plate of spaghetti sandwiched between them. Larry nudged a meatball toward Coffee, and the pixelated face blushed.

Del and Snacks let out a conjoined, "Aww."

"This is not cute!" Lonnie stormed back into the apartment and rifled through several of the shelves. "Ah, here it is." She retrieved the phone book. Generally, touching the phone book would be a nonissue, however, it currently propped up a shelf containing several glass bits and bobbles.

Kale dove forward and propped up the shelf before it completely fell over. The only thing he could find to take the spot of the phone book was an empty can. He backed away slowly, holding his arms outstretched as if that would actually do something. It seemed solid enough for now.

"Woah there!" Snacks rescued the pizza box as Lonnie shoved aside everything on the counter to make way for the phone book.

Lonnie remained intently focused, but she snapped her fingers at Del. "Del, run a scan for dragonkin in our universe."

Del crossed her arms and raised an eyebrow.

Lonnie sighed and glanced up. "Sorry. Del, would you *please* run a scan for dragonkin in our universe?"

Del winked at her and retrieved her phone. "Since I don't know how to do that, I'm just gonna Schgoogle '*Dragons near me.*'"

Snacks handed her his phone. "Oh, use the app Treasure-Hoard...though it's more for...uh..."

Del read aloud, "*Find sexy dragons in your area.*"

They all stopped, even Lonnie, to look up at Snacks.

He tugged at his collar a bit. "What? I listen to a lot of podcasts! I've never even been in a dragon universe for longer than a layover so it's not like I've actually—"

"—You have a profile!?" Del exclaimed as she swiped through the app and bolted through the apartment, reading aloud.

Snacks chased her and snatched the phone back, but in the process his finger slid across the screen. The "*It's A Match!*" screen popped up. He turned a bright shade of red.

Del put a hand on his shoulder. "You're welcome."

Lonnie's train of thought left the station. "Based on the prevalence of dragons that would be necessary for Snacks to get a match that quickly—"

"—Hey!"

She didn't seem to notice him. "We can assume that not only does our universe now have many dragons, but they've completely assimilated into society." Lonnie dog-eared a page of the phone book and closed it. Then, as she lifted the book upwards, it expanded as if thousands of pages were being inserted one at a time. It rose a foot before she opened it and continued to flip through.

Kale, sensing Lonnie was in one of her too-focused-to-talk states, approached Del. "So, what happens if our universe now has dragons?" It was a sentence he never thought he'd say.

Del shrugged. "Nothing that I can think of..."

"Keep in mind that her business thrives on death and destruction," Lonnie said, monotone.

"Not true!" Del argued. "We moved 'destruction' to a whole other building. They legally operate as a business independent from our own!"

"My mistake," Lonnie sighed as she slammed the phone book shut. "It's no use."

"Whatever it is, I'm sure you'll figure it out," Del replied.

"That's the thing. I've never heard of two universes colliding like this before. Except in cases of massive universal collapse, of course." Lonnie cracked open a beer.

Those last words caused Kale to perk up. "And by that...you mean...?"

Lonnie snapped her fingers. "Just like that, a whole universe down the drain." She made a fart noise with her lips and sat on the couch, putting her feet up on the coffee table. "But we're still here, and since I don't know how to fix this, or if there's anything even to fix, the safest and most logical thing we can do is all stay together and wait this out."

"Right, seeya!" Snacks popped on his coat and wound up to kick the front door.

"Where are you going at this hour?" Kale rose quickly to open it for him.

"...I...have a meeting." Snacks twiddled his thumbs.

Del smiled. "You have a date with a dragon!"

"I...I..." Snacks said, flustered. "I'm doing reconnaissance so we can figure out the thing Lonnie was talking about with the world imploding or whatever. Good day!" He waited for Kale to open the door before exiting swiftly.

Del followed Snacks out the door and knocked on her own apartment door.

Lonnie rolled her eyes. "It's a waste of time, Coffee won't open—"

The door to Lonnie and Del's apartment swung open. Del was greeted by a welcoming robotic voice before the door promptly closed and ten different locks clicked into place. Coffee's arm reached under the door and taped a hand-drawn sign that said, "*No Elonifreds Allowed*" to the outside.

Where most people would ask, Lonnie told Kale, "I'm staying here tonight."

She patted an empty spot on the couch as Kale left the door ajar for Snacks. Silently, she found the remote, right where it should be, and flipped on the television.

"Ugh," Lonnie started. "Another reality show. I swear, they throw these things together in a week."

"Up next," an announcer's magnificent throaty voice boomed over footage of a figure running through the forest. "A historical documentary about the chosen one." Kale watched a familiar crowd of peasants look on with awe as a seven-foot lumberjack pulled a sword from a stone. "A story...with a whole lot of attitude."

One of those abrupt record scratch sound effects played as it cut to an interview with a peasant. "Sorry? He's not Sorry."

Then there was a fast-paced montage of the chosen one slaughtering armies, beheading kings, and drinking mimosas as the announcer spoke. "Coming soon: Real Chosen Ones of The Kingdom of Fendaris."

Kale and Lonnie looked at each other with wide-eyed excitement.

Lonnie pointed enthusiastically. "Did you see that?! My arm was in one of the shots!"

"Well, we have to watch it," Kale reached for the last slice of pizza. But at the same time, so did Lonnie. They touched hands, and both lingered just a second longer than necessary.

As they pulled away and locked eyes, Lonnie smiled at Kale. "Hey—"

"—WE INTERRUPT THIS BROADCAST FOR AN EMERGENCY ANNOUNCEMENT!" A suave anchor with floofy hair sat at a desk. "EMERGENCY" flashed across the screen. It was alarming enough that both sat up immediately.

The anchor straightened their papers. "We've just received a report that earlier today, I adopted this puppy, and I need everyone to see how cute it is." A justifiably cute puppy appeared on the screen. The anchor continued in a monotone voice that reminded Kale of 1950s radio. "I have named him Sprinkles. Here's another picture. And another." The anchor turned to another camera and touched their ear. "We're getting reports that Sprinkles is a very good boy who likes walkies and getting his tum tum scratched."

Upon hearing "scratched", Dog appeared and curled up between Kale and Lonnie like an expectant Venus flytrap.

"We will continue to bring you updates as we receive them. In other news, a universal tariff on coconuts was heard and passed by the Galactic Council. Finally...hmm...is there any other news?" the anchor asked off-screen.

"They really are desperate for views, aren't they?" Lonnie judged at the television.

"Oh, right," the anchor said nonchalantly. "Earlier today, Universe Dragon Balls, which is responsible for the invention of yoga balls for dragons, went missing. We have no further information, but if anyone sees Universe Dragon Balls, please tell it to return home." A graphic of the universe on the back of a milk carton flashed across the screen.

The two sat up once again, much to Dog's annoyance.

"I never thought I'd say this, but broadcast television has actually helped us!" Lonnie hopped up and went to the phone book with Kale in tow.

The anchor continued. "Again, we have no information other than the universe is missing. However, our team of investigative experts, an ogre and two unpaid interns, has concluded that this was an act of terrorism. They've also unearthed that the terrorist responsible is this creature..."

Kale glanced back at the screen and did a double take. He tapped Lonnie on the shoulder and both stared at Kale's face with a large "WANTED" sign under it.

"While we have no evidence that this person is an actual terrorist, this blurry security camera does show them walking down the street." They rolled a video that was so blurry they had to squint to see it was humanoid. "We know nothing about this terrorist mastermind, however, our sources are guessing this awful piece of garbage terrorist is called 'Kale.'"

"I...I didn't..." Kale looked frantically between the television and Lonnie.

"We have more information coming in now." The anchor was

handed a crumpled napkin with some writing on it. "Yes, our sources say that since watching our program, the Galactic Police have issued an arrest warrant for Kale. I think I speak for all of us when I say: let's get back to talking about Sprinkles."

Lonnie turned off the television.

Kale felt queasy. "I have no idea what they're talking about. You have to believe me!"

"Well, duh. You're too dumb to–I mean, I was with your unconscious body when that happened, so it couldn't've been you." Lonnie leafed through the phone book.

Before Kale could respond, the door burst open and Del entered, visibly disturbed. "This is bad! Real bad!"

Kale backed away and held up his hands defensively. "Del, I didn't do it, I swear!"

"What? I didn't think you started the coconut tariff in the first place...but now I do..." She pointed a finger at him confusedly.

"I...didn't...terrorism," he spat out.

Del groaned and looked up at the ceiling. "Ugh! Can we not talk about *you* for a minute?! Look, congrats on destroying a universe or whatever, but this coconut tariff threatens my job. Could you be a bit more supportive?" Del grabbed the last slice of pizza and tried to smother her anxiety with it.

Kale looked for help from Lonnie, but she was deep in the phone book. "I'm...sorry, Del. Wanna talk about it?"

Del sighed and sprawled over the couch. "Since I work in the Coconut Division of Falling Object Deaths, this could mean massive layoffs! No one's gonna kill with coconuts anymore!" Del shoved her face into a pillow.

Kale sat next to her. "Listen, it's pretty obvious that I don't know anything about anything, but..." Kale struggled to find something to say. "...But...coconuts...will always...kill people?" he mumbled.

Del looked up at him with a sad glare, then hugged him. "Oh Kale, you always know what to say!"

Kale, in the third-most intelligent idea of his lifetime, decided to quit while he was ahead.

Del wiped away a tear. "Now, tell me all about how you destroyed that universe."

"I...I didn't."

"Don't be modest." Del's phone chimed. "Oh! That's probably my friends from the Cataclysm Division, thanking *you* for the overtime!"

Kale tried to object, but Lonnie cut him off.

"–Found it! And he didn't do it, Del."

Kale was relieved. "Fantastic, so I shouldn't worry about the Galactic Police coming after me?"

"You most definitely should! In fact, they'll likely round up all the versions of you and toss y'all into a prison universe." Lonnie whacked the fuse box a few times and some lights flashed. "That's it! Sorry Del, but your friends aren't getting any overtime. Universe Dragon Balls is fine, it's just...*nested*...for lack of a better term, with our universe."

"That's...a good thing?" Kale said with all the confidence of an English major.

"...And we may have caused it." Lonnie finished a beer and crushed the can in her hand.

"Neat!" Del replied. "Then why did I get an alert..." She delved deep into her phone.

"Hmm," Lonnie puzzled to herself. "So, the Multiverse was leaking, and in our attempt to get home, we may have spread that leak across the Multiverse."

"How far?" Del tapped furiously on her phone.

"...Seven?" Lonnie said hesitantly. It was one of the few times she actually appeared unnerved.

Del froze and looked up. "SEVEN!?"

"Don't worry! I have a plan. All we need to do is run the Z-Control protocol." She pointed to Del. "Tell Snacks to get back here as soon as possible. We need to get all of us in one place, or the leak will continue to spread and destroy...well, everything."

Throughout this exchange, Kale had picked up Dog and paced around the room nervously.

"About that," Del looked at her phone. "...Do we need *all* of Snacks or will several pieces work? Like, hypothetically, if someone's requested to murder him, would that be good or...*not* good?"

"What?!" Kale asked.

"I have Reapr alerts set for all my friends to make sure you get the best death possible!" Del poked her phone into Kale's face. "Look, I don't want Snacks to die either, but the killer does have 4.9 stars and some pretty excellent reviews."

Kale grabbed a coat from the rack. "How long until it happens?"

"Results may vary, but sometime in the next five to ten minutes-ish..."

She looked up and Kale was already out the door and down the stairs. "Kale! Where are you going?"

In a moment of mild coolness, Kale looked her dead in the eye. "I'm gonna save my best friend."

Unfortunately, he then missed a step and tripped down the remaining few stairs.

Lonnie poked her head out. "I meant...like, where, physically, is Snacks? Also, you're wearing my coat!"

Kale knew just the place.

# NINE

## On Takeout

---

Kale panted as he arrived at his favorite restaurant, The Dumpling Garage. It was one of those hole-in-the-wall restaurants where the only entrance was through a crumbling hole in the wall.

But before Kale entered, he noticed another hole entrance. It was much larger, almost dragon-sized.

The interior was elegant, like a vast ballroom. Kale remembered it having barstools and a counter, but somehow also remembered this room. Thinking too hard about it gave him a brain freeze. Technically, there weren't many creatures in the room, but several scattered dragons made it feel quite full.

"Hello, table for one?" the hostess asked as Kale impolitely rushed past her.

He saw Snacks at a table opposite a crimson dragon and grabbed his arm. "Snacks, we gotta go. Now!"

Moments before, Snacks had been thoroughly enjoying himself. Startled, he didn't budge. "Kale? What are you...I'm a bit engaged at the moment." Snacks turned to the crimson dragon who delicately used chopsticks to pop dumplings into its fanged maw. "I'm so sorry about this." He turned back to Kale. "Whatever it is, it can wait."

Kale looked around the room, paranoid. He wondered if the killer was someone in this room...or even across the table from them. "Snacks, look at me, you're in great danger. We have to go right now." He leaned in closer, "Someone here wants to kill you."

"And?"

Kale blinked at him, unsure what else to say.

"Kale, it's safe to say a lot of people want to kill me." Snacks turned to the crimson dragon, "Again, I'm so sorry about this. Do you mind if I look at my phone? I know it's rude on a date. By the way, Kale, meet Revinath. Revinath, meet Kale."

"Hello." Kale waved awkwardly.

The dragon made a series of friendly roars.

"She asked what you do for a living." Snacks didn't look up from his phone.

"I...I'm sorta between jobs right now...yourself?" Kale didn't know what to do as Revinath responded with several long, guttural roars.

Snacks chuckled. "Sorry, inside joke. She designs treasure hoard mattresses and actually just got accepted to a master's program in princess guardianship."

Revinath blushed and waved a talon at Snacks while she roared lightly, almost a purr.

"Don't be so modest! It's a great program, and you should be proud."

Revinath smiled sweetly and gave Snacks what could only be described as bedroom eyes.

Seeing Kale's persistence, Snacks sighed and scanned the room until he made eye contact with a lone blonde woman reading a book at a nearby table. "Excuse me?"

She looked up. "Yes?"

"Were you planning on serial killing me in the next few minutes?"

"Yes I was. Well, I was actually going to wait until your date was over. It's very rude to interrupt such things." The blonde serial killer glared at Kale.

"Of course. Thank you for that. Any chance we could move it to next week?"

"Yeah, sure thing. I can do Monday or Wednesday."

"Oof, I'm busy both those days. Friday?"

"Can't do Friday, I have a friend's bridal shower."

"Those are fun. How about the following week?"

"It's a little hazy because I'm supposed to kill this other person, but they're really good at escaping and the buddy system. How about we play it by ear, and I just kill you sometime in the next few weeks? Here." She took out a blood-red business card and handed it to Snacks.

"That's perfect. Thank you!" Snacks raised a glass to her before he acknowledged Kale. "Satisfied? Can I get back to my date now, please?"

Before Kale could awkwardly fingerguns and shuffle away, a triumphant voice boomed behind him. "Do not worry, chosen one! I shall aid you in your quest!" Larry flew through the air, "Huza–AHH!" He bumped into a chair, which sent him spinning wildly through the room.

Kale felt an impact. He looked down and saw Larry embedded in his shoulder.

"...Whoopsie," Larry said, his voice muffled through the shoulder meat. "I'm so sorry. I swear this never happens."

Kale, through an enormous amount of willpower, did not scream, though nearly every eye in the restaurant was on him.

"I guess you should ice that..." Snacks shooed Kale away, but then his eyes narrowed to a television in the corner. After 59 minutes of dog photos, Kale's face had reappeared.

Murmurs and mumblings spread through the room as Kale ducked out a side exit.

"Larry...can you please...no longer be inside me?" Kale gasped as he staggered back to his apartment.

"I appear to have pierced a major artery, and the pull-out method will not be effective...as you will bleed out in forty seconds. Would you still like me to continue?"

"No, stay put." Kale heard sirens approach and ducked through a back alley.

Larry hummed and made little beatboxing sounds as if any silence would kill them both. "Just FYI, chosen one. It feels really great to be inside you. I've been in a lot of people, and you have an excellent body temperature."

"T-thank you?" Kale replied.

"You are very welcome," Larry said with a tablespoon of awkwardness. The sword then doubled down and recounted stories of people and monsters he didn't like, mainly merpeople and those who frequently lose online games, as both were particularly salty.

The two finally arrived at their apartment. Kale trudged up the stairs and meekly raised his arm to push open Lonnie and Del's door. The locks appeared to have been melted off.

"I know, I know." Coffee hung glumly from the ceiling. "You're not mad, you're just disappointed."

"I am *both* of those things! So help me, I will melt you down to scrap if you do something like this one more time." Lonnie pounded away on the buttons at the arcade machine.

It was a very tense moment as Coffee drifted closer to Lonnie with big, pixelated puppy dog eyes. Coffee then extended a finger and poked Lonnie on the nose: "Boop." The long arm glided away across the ceiling as Coffee giggled.

Lonnie fumed and grabbed a blowtorch. Del watched all this, excitedly eating popcorn.

"Ahem," Larry said as Kale bled profusely in the doorway.

Immediately, everyone turned, but Coffee glided over in an instant. "Danger detected. Initiating emergency medicine protocols." About a dozen sharp blades and needles extended from Coffee's various ports and crevasses.

"Coffee, cease!" Lonnie yelled as Coffee reluctantly put the tools away.

"Are you alright?" Coffee asked.

"I'm fine," Kale lied, his face becoming pale as he leaned on the doorframe. "Snacks is safe and I–"

"–Sir. Please end your vocal functions," Coffee interrupted. "Larry? Are you alright?"

After he paused for dramatic effect, Larry let out a stifled cough, despite not having a mouth. "Me? Oh, I'm fine. You should see the other guy."

Coffee swooned. "You're so brave! Hold on, I'll cut you out of there in just a moment." A large, spinning saw extended toward Kale's shoulder.

As Kale recoiled, Lonnie shook her head and tapped a button on her wrist tablet. Coffee froze, the saw blade inches from Kale's shoulder as he sidestepped into the apartment.

"Hold on! Hold on!" Del said frantically. Kale thought she was reaching for a first aid kit, when she pulled out a plastic sheet and laid it down below him. "It's a new carpet."

Kale leaned on a barstool as Lonnie examined Kale's wound and arm. Her thumb lightly stroked her chin. "Damn, it's completely ruined. We'll have to cut it off."

"Wait, hold on!" Kale's eyes went wide as Lonnie approached him with scissors.

She then proceeded to cut the jacket off him. "You owe me a coat."

"Right...sorry–OW!" Kale flinched as she reached out slowly and poked the wound.

"Right. Removing Larry could cause you serious damage. I think he's gotta stay in forever."

"I hope you like podcasts!" Larry exclaimed happily.

Kale winced as the adrenaline trickled away. "Can't you just, like, use that staple gun thing from before?"

"Oh, you mean the one you and Snacks used *all* my charges for?" she replied snarkily. "Nope, we should see a real doctor for this one. I'll set up a portal to a place with Multiversal healthcare." Lonnie went to her arcade cabinet and pushed buttons until a metal doorframe in the living room glowed blue.

A few seconds later, it let out a sputtering noise that slowly devolved into the sound of long wet flatulence. The blue light faded.

"Del? You paid the portal bill, right?"

Del's eyes rose to the ceiling. "Either that or the gas bill. I forget which."

"Hold on." Lonnie examined the doorframe, and there was gunk around the edges. "Someone's purposely clogging our way out of here..."

There was a loud knock outside the door. "Galactic Police! Open up!"

Everyone froze. Lonnie tapped her wrist computer and pulled up a live feed to the hallway between their two apartments. The space was filled with dozens of futuristically-armored officers. They proceeded to kick down the door to Kale's apartment, leaving Lonnie and Del's door untouched.

The sound of the door crashing caused all of them to jump, except Kale, who, after spending a decent amount of time with Snacks, was used to doors being kicked down. Even Larry wiggled a bit, much to Kale's dismay.

The officers poured into Kale's apartment and tore it apart. "Hey, why do you have cameras in my apartment?" Kale asked, before he realized Lonnie had detached the tablet from her wrist and was now moving quickly through the apartment.

She pushed aside a bookshelf and revealed a small cubby with a bug-out bag. As Lonnie stuffed items into the pack, Del opened her purse and waved her hands around. A dark energy like black fire swirled around objects in the room as they floated into her purse. She paused as DVDs flew off the shelf.

"Whose copy of *SpaceBop* is whose?" Del held up two DVDs with cover art of cube-shaped spaceships.

"I don't own a copy of *SpaceBop*." Lonnie used an electric screwdriver to open the arcade cabinet before reaching inside and yanking out a little box with wires connected, much like she was pulling out a heart.

"What? So I have *two* copies?"

"You must. I've never seen it."

Del stopped packing. "You've *never* seen *SpaceBop*?"

"No, I'm not really into epic fantasy."

"Guffaw!" Del exclaimed. "Alright, stop what you're doing. We're watching *SpaceBop*." Del went to the TV and put in the DVD.

"I don't think we have time right now," Lonnie said as Kale nodded in agreement. He flipped through the cameras as the Galactic Police ransacked his apartment to no avail. A few of the officers still outside glanced at Lonnie and Del's apartment curiously.

"Oh hush. You're always making excuses." Del took a glowing purple crystal from her pocket and smashed it on the floor.

Kale blinked, and the two of them were gone. Then he jumped as he heard their voices behind him. "I just didn't think the laser swords were feasible, that's all! Like, how do they just keep going? Shouldn't they have to stop at some point?!"

Del rinsed out a bowl of popcorn kernels. "It's just one of those things you just accept exists in the world. Don't question it."

"I agree with Elonifred," Larry chimed in. "I like the rest of the series, but the laser swords set unrealistic expectations of the enchanted weapon community. At least after the recent films there was a counter-movement of blade positivity."

"Huh, I never considered that," Del replied thoughtfully. "Also, I guess the time crystals that allow me to freeze time once in my life have worn off. What were we doing before this?"

Suddenly, the door burst open and the Galactic Police rushed in. They yelled for everyone to put their hands up.

The crew complied, and the room was secured.

A figure pushed through the soldiers as the sound of spurs drew closer. Unlike the other officers, this one wore a sturdy black cowboy hat made of metal or perhaps a thick plastic. Somehow, the fact that it was secured around his head with a strap and buckle didn't lessen the intimidation as he approached.

"Well, well, well, well, well, well, well...what have we here? We're looking for a terrorist mastermind. Have you seen this person?" The Cowboy held up a sketch of Kale and showed it around. No one spoke as he held the sketch up to Kale's face.

Kale gulped as the Cowboy looked back and forth between the sketch and Kale.

The Cowboy groaned. "It's not him. This one has a sword sticking out of him."

Most of the Galactic Police nodded along, however one raised their hand. "Sir, that sketch doesn't show the shoulders, so it's possible the sword was inserted recently!" The rest of the officers nodded along.

"Fine," the Cowboy said after some long moments of consideration. "What're all your names?"

He pointed to Lonnie first. She glanced around the room quickly. "I'm...daisy...flower...berg...stein...plant..."

The Cowboy nodded and wrote it down in his notepad. "Daisy Flowerbergsteinplant, alright. You?" He shifted over to Del.

As he did this, Lonnie whispered to Kale, "Just pick any generic name."

Del eyed the ceiling "Uh...my name is...Sna...akes...Snakes...first name...One...Hundred."

He squinted at her. "So, you're saying your name is *One Hundred Snakes*?"

Del nodded.

The Cowboy stared her down before he wrote it on his notepad. "Alright then, and you?"

"John Smith," Kale said, confident for maybe the first time in his life.

The Cowboy paused and looked up. "John...Smith?"

"Yup," Kale replied.

A murmur spread through the room of officers, and the Cowboy stepped closer to him. "That's an unusual name. Are you from this universe?"

Kale nodded. The Cowboy looked him up and down. "I know a fake name when I hear it! Arrest this person!"

As the Galactic Police strong-armed Kale and led him out, the Cowboy tilted his helmet to the others. "Flowerbergsteinplant, Snakes, I regret to inform you this person is a terrorist, and we are placing him under arrest."

"Oh my!" Del fanned herself and pretended to faint, trust falling into Lonnie's open arms.

"Golly gee willikers," Lonnie started in a monotone. "What's the sentencing on that?"

The last thing Kale saw was the smile of the Cowboy. "Execution."

# TEN

## Bad Cop, Bad Cop

---

W hen the bag was taken off his head, Kale found himself in a dark room. The table in front of him was grey with rough edges...and, from the feel of it, his chair was made of a similar material. He was relieved to see Larry had been removed, and he was bandaged up, but the wound still ached.

The Cowboy took a seat across from him. He took a digital timer with menacing red numbers and placed it on the table. Kale watched it start at fifteen minutes and tick down.

"So, how'd ya do it, kid?" The Cowboy kicked his feet up on the metal table which remained firmly bolted to the floor. Kale gulped, fiercely intimidated by the ambience. "What leads a man to–"

"–GREEEEEEEEEEEEEE."

Kale looked over his shoulder to see a larger man behind a desk removing a pencil from an ancient sharpener.

The Cowboy bit his tongue and turned his attention back to Kale. "We know you–"

"–GREEEEEEEEEEEEEEE." The man, who had a recent mustard stain on his tie, sharpened another pencil.

"Wixby!" the Cowboy shouted. "Must you sharpen your pencils right at this moment?"

"...Sarge says this is my space too! But I won't sharpen any more unless these two break."

"Thank you," the Cowboy sighed and turned back to Kale. "We...are having a bit of an issue with space. Now, where were we?"

A light sizzling sound and the smell of cooking meat wafted through the interrogation room. Wixby had taken out a small grilling station, a miniature version of something you'd find in a convenience store, and cooked hot dogs.

"...We know you've been traveling through the Multiverse without a permit, and we–"

"–*Hi there! Welcome to my channel where I teach you how to cook the perfect hot dogs. To start...*"

The Cowboy's head slowly craned over to Wixby as he studied the screen scrupulously. "Wixby, you know how to make hot dogs. You make them every single day."

Wixby pointed to the screen. "But the title says this is the *best* way to cook hot dogs..."

The Cowboy motioned for Wixby to put on headphones. Wixby did, but not before stating how he didn't like how they felt on his ears.

"We also found traces of an unauthorized portal in your residence. How do you expl–"

"–Ha!" Wixby shouted.

The Cowboy waited a moment. "...How do you expla–"

"–HAHA!" Wixby pointed at the screen.

The Cowboy waited yet another long moment. "...How do you explain these–"

"–BAHAHAHAHAHA!" Wixby chortled at the screen.

"Wixby...Wixby!" the Cowboy shouted to no response. He threw a pen across Wixby's face.

"WHAT?" Wixby yelled. "SORRY, I CAN'T HEAR YOU. THESE ARE NOISE-CANCELING HEADPHONES."

The Cowboy, whose teeth audibly ground, made a dramatic motion for Wixby to remove the headphones. Wixby did, and the Cowboy summoned every bit of patience he had remaining. "Wixby, can't you see we're in the middle of something pretty important?"

The gears turned in Wixby's head. "Oh...*OH*! Say no more."

The Cowboy relaxed a bit and turned back to Kale. "And we also have video of you trespassing in a private universe..."

Wixby placed a hot dog in front of each of them. He stood over them with a near-empty bottle of ketchup. "PTHHHBTTTT...PTHH-HBTTTT...PTTTHHHHHHHHBBBTTTTTTTT."

Kale had never seen a look of such anger as the one the Cowboy wore now.

"Oh...do you not like ketchup?"

The Cowboy gripped the table with enough force to dent the metal. "Thank you, Wixby. No more interruptions from now on, capiche?"

"DiGiorno." Wixby flashed a thumbs-up and quietly went to his desk. He filled out paperwork. The Cowboy smiled and waited for Kale to say something.

It was common knowledge that one should never talk to the Galactic Police, but Kale did not possess such wisdom. As the big red numbers ticked down, he felt very compelled to say something, anything, to break the silence. "Look, this all started when–"

"–GREEEEEEEEEEEEEE."

Kale and the Cowboy looked over to see Wixby sharpening pencils, again.

"GREEEEEEEEEEEEEEE." He looked up and smiled at the two of them. "I just keep breakin' 'em. What a klutz I am!"

A vein popped on the Cowboy's forehead, and Kale thought his noggin might explode. "I swear, the next person who interrupts–"

Suddenly, the door flew open with such force that everyone turned. A gloved hand extended to keep the door from ricocheting back. The figure wore a grey suit and thick glasses, their mane of hair tied back in a magnificent man bun. It was none other than Knightly. Snacks Knightly.

"Court-appointed lawyer." Snacks waltzed into the room. He set down a briefcase on the table. He extended a hand to Kale and winked. "I'll be representing you. My name's Snakes. *Two Hundred* Snakes."

"Ah," the Cowboy said knowingly. "Any relation to One Hundred Snakes?"

"No," Snacks replied coolly. "It's a very common name." Snacks opened the briefcase so only he and Kale could see it. It was empty other than a few candy bars. "Hmm...yes...I see..." He pretended to leaf through papers. "Well, clearly, my client is innocent."

"I can see wounds that line up with Multiverse exploration." The Cowboy pointed at him.

"My client has a cat. These deep impalations could easily be from an annoyed tabby."

"You're saying a cat created that hole in his shoulder?!"

"It's certainly possible," Snacks countered.

"Oh, it's true!" Wixby chimed in. "My cat, Sir Flufferbutter, loves to get frisky!"

Snacks and Wixby continued back and forth until the Cowboy slammed his fist on the table. "We just removed the weapon from his shoulder!"

Snacks clicked open his briefcase again and pretended to scribble a note. "So, you admit you removed the blade in question from my client's shoulder without written permission?"

"He was bleeding out! I get what you're about, tryin' ta give me the ol' reach-around!"

Kale coughed to stifle his laughter. "I think you mean *runaround*."

All the others looked at him with quizzical eyes.

"The sex thing?" Wixby asked.

Snacks whispered in Kale's ear, clarifying that he was in a universe where those two words were reversed. He also ominously warned Kale to never ask for dressing on the side here.

"Clearly, my client has suffered severe, dum-dum-inducing trauma because of this sword removal...but that's no problem for the Galactic Police when you can just fudge some paperwork. Isn't that right?"

The Cowboy smiled and leaned back.

"But I think you'll have trouble explaining why you interfered with the *Galactic Endangered Species Act, Part Nine: This Time We're Serious.*" Snacks once more opened the briefcase. Now, a paper, heavy with long words, sat there waiting for him. He handed it to the Cowboy and pointed to a highlighted section.

A look of muffled concern hit the Cowboy right on the nose. "...*The Galactic Council hereby grants full protective rights to the endangered species of...enchanted weapons*?!"

Snacks reached out and turned the timer toward him for a moment. Time was running out. He slid it back before the Cowboy noticed.

"Oooo! They got us good!" Wixby said jubilantly.

"I wonder how it's gonna look when your station gets charged with wrenching a defenseless enchanted weapon from its home?" Snacks went on to list the fines and punishments for crimes against enchanted weapons.

As this happened, the Cowboy stood and walked to a locker. He pulled out Larry and unlocked an adorably tiny set of handcuffs around the hilt.

"So, I guess the ball's in your court..." Snacks leaned back in his chair smugly as he bit into the hotdog still in front of Kale.

The Cowboy paused for a moment, then stabbed Kale in the shoulder with Larry.

Kale screamed into his shirt.

Snacks looked up at the Cowboy with a tinge of admiration. "Well played."

"Uh, I think it was the other shoulder...." Wixby said before he fearfully returned to typing on the loudest keyboard in the Multiverse.

"Right, whoopsie." The Cowboy reached over and pulled Larry from Kale's shoulder, then stabbed it right into the other. Again, Kale screamed into his jacket (technically, Lonnie's jacket). The Cowboy squinted at the other wound. "You know, I think I liked it better in the other shoulder."

Snacks nodded to him. "Yeah, it just seems out of place on this side."

"How about we get a second sword and put it in the other shoulder so it's even?" the Cowboy suggested earnestly.

"I will confirm with my client." Snacks turned to Kale, who recoiled and tried to stop the bleeding.

"Absolutely not!" Kale yelled.

"My client will consider this," Snacks told the Cowboy.

A little chime went off at Wixby's desk and he turned to the Cowboy. "Oh! I set a timer for—"

"—WIXBY!" the Cowboy yelled. "Whatever you're going to say, I don't want to hear it. You've done nothing but ruin this interrogation. NOT. ANOTHER. PEEP!"

Wixby sullenly turned back toward his computer. He put on headphones and everyone collectively ignored that he was listening to sad 80s power ballads.

The Cowboy turned the timer toward them. It ticked down with just one minute left. "Now, is your client pleading to this lesser charge of *accidental* Multiverse collision, or are we charging him with full-blown Multiverse *terrorism?*"

Kale looked between Snacks and the Cowboy as they stared each other down for thirty seconds straight. But the moment the timer hit thirty seconds, Snacks rose and reached out a hand. "It was a pleasure speaking with you." He gestured for the Cowboy to unlock Kale's handcuffs.

"Still twenty seconds on the clock. Maybe I'll double the charge," the Cowboy said smugly.

"Actually," Wixby interjected. "When you were distracted, he added thirty seconds to the timer, so fifteen minutes have already passed. I set my own timer to give you a heads-up, but then you didn't want me to talk..."

A look of pure annoyance and fury spread across the Cowboy's face as the timer finally hit zero and beeped loudly. He reluctantly unlocked the handcuffs and Snacks led Kale out of the room. Snacks paused at the exit and turned back. "Oh, and Wixby? Great hot dogs." He took a bite and closed the door.

Snacks confidently led a very bloody Kale through the precinct. "I don't understand what just happened...even more than usual."

"If they don't charge you with a crime in the first fifteen minutes, you get to leave. That's like, the first thing they teach you in Multiverse law school."

"I didn't know you were a Multiverse lawyer."

"I'm not, but you can pretty much sneak in *anywhere* if you wear a suit." Kale only now realized that Snacks, while projecting a high level of confidence, was nervous as they approached the exit.

They were just a few steps away from freedom when a loud voice called out from behind them, "Hey you! Stop right there!" A gruff-looking officer raised a pistol toward them.

As Kale tried to put his hands up, Snacks yanked him out the door and they bolted down the city street.

Gunshots echoed behind them as bullets whizzed past their heads. They ducked into an alleyway.

"How did they figure it out?!" Snacks murmured. "I thought that plan was foolproof..."

* * *

BACK IN FRONT OF THE PRECINCT, THE OFFICER'S HEAD DROOPED. Another officer wearing a party hat poked his head out. "Did ya get 'em?"

The two walked back inside. The room was now packed with officers in party hats. They held a sheet cake that read, "*Congratulations! You're our one billionth customer!*"

"Did you give 'em the free bullets?"

The sad officer nodded. "I tried, but I'm just not a very good shot, Sarge..."

"You'll get 'em next time, champ. We'll just have a party for the one billionth and first customer...and hey, free bullets for everyone!" Sarge fired his gun in the air, everyone did. It was a warm, happy moment. They passed out salads for the rabbit-folk.

"Hey, can I get dressing on the side?" one of the new recruits asked sheepishly. The room went silent as the others turned to him uncomfortably.

Immediately, the new recruit shrunk down as the hulking Sarge stepped forward. "What'd you say?"

The new recruit gulped.

The Sarge cracked his knuckles. "Time for you to learn how the Galactic Police deal with your type...." The Sarge put on his spectacles and wrote on a whiteboard, "*Appropriate language in the workplace.*" He walked up, right into the new recruits face. "Now...let's unpack this."

# ELEVEN

## Love Wins

---

"**D**on't stop running! If they catch us it'll be nothing but torture...and not the whimsical, hilarious kind previously featured. Like bloody, trauma-inducing scenes that make this adventure go from mostly PG-13 to a solid R!" Snacks yelled as he ducked through alleys with Kale in tow.

They finally stopped several blocks away and got into a clear elevator. They leaned back and caught their breath as it slowly ascended.

Snacks retrieved a roll of duct tape and plastered it over the wound currently not occupied by a sword. The bleeding slowed and clotted.

"Thanks," Kale said. "For the rescue, I mean. How'd the rest of the date go?"

"She tried to eat me."

"...Oh, sorry."

"What? Oh, it's all good, it was consensual. We're having dinner together again next week." Snacks smiled like a goofy kid in love. "But even so, thanks for coming to my rescue," he chuckled. "Had I known *you* were in trouble, I would've ended the date early, brometheus."

"You'd do that for me, broseidon?"

"That's what bros do."

"Bros?" Kale held out a fist bump.

"Bros." Snacks pounded Kale's arm with such might his wound reopened.

Remembering he had been impaled, Kale tapped on the gem and unmuted Larry, who let out a gasp of air. "OH YEAH! I forgot how good it feels to be stabbed into someone! Yippee!" Larry vibrated, very much to Kale's dismay.

"You wanna stab? Go stab!" Snacks waved his hand in front of Larry and then pretended to throw an invisible ball or severed head outward. Immediately, Larry shot out of Kale's arm and shattered part of the glass elevator door. He soared high over the city as Snacks taped over Kale's exposed wound.

"Here." Snacks retrieved a lollipop from his briefcase and handed it to Kale.

"Is this a magical healing candy?" Kale stuck it in his mouth.

Snacks paused. "Sure!"

Kale didn't believe him, but it did make the about-to-die feeling drift away a little.

Snacks whistled and pulled out a raw steak from his briefcase.

"Ohboyohboyohboy..." a quiet voice grew louder and louder. "OHBOYOHBOYOHBOY!" Larry shot into the elevator and skewered the steak into the wall. The sword laughed maniacally as it tore the meat apart. Larry then stopped abruptly. "I...I'm sorry...I don't know what came over me." He feigned a light British accent to appear more poised and knowledgeable, something we can all relate to, I'm sure.

All three of them let out a sigh as they rose higher over the vast city. It looked like any other city to Kale, except cars had been replaced with flying carpets. That explained how he had gotten a bit of rug burn while being transported here, and why the journey had felt so billowy.

The elevator opened to a rooftop garden. Kale liked plants, he found they were exceptional conversationalists.

Once again, they moved with vigor. Snacks pulled Kale over to the edge and already Kale's palms felt sweaty.

"Right, now we jump." Snacks said frankly as he scanned the horizon and retrieved a Rubik's Cube from his briefcase.

"What?!" Kale peered over the side and immediately retracted as a big gust smacked him in the face.

"We need to build up enough momentum to make the jump into the next universe." Snacks pulled hidden straps from his briefcase to turn it into a backpack.

Something about Snacks' mannerisms made Kale question him. "Snacks, be real with me. Do we really have to jump off this building?"

"It'll be fine. A portal will open right before we hit the ground."

Kale crossed his arms. "Seriously?"

"Do you see another way out of here?" Snacks motioned to the rooftop garden.

"...Alright," Kale said hesitantly.

"Great. You go first, and I'll be right behind you."

"Why do I have to go first?"

"Oh, did you want to close the portal behind us? Is that in your skill set?" Snacks said with an extra tablespoon of sass. "Do you want to configure our coordinates?" Snacks held out the Rubik's Cube, but Kale didn't accept it.

"Fine." Kale approached the edge and turned back to Snacks, who flashed him a thumbs-up. Kale swayed back and forth, ready to leap. *Three...two...one*–"Nope. I can't do it." Kale walked away from the edge, his stomach in knots. Snacks still fiddled with the Rubik's Cube.

"Just do it! Our lives depend on this!"

"You're serious? You're not messing with me?"

"Kale, why would I do that? Now hurry up. Time is of the essence!"

Kale wound up once more. This time, he let the fear wash over him. He accepted all he'd been through, everything he'd survived, and he took a step forward as a man free from his own mental prison.

"–HA! Gotcha!" Snacks pulled him back onto the rooftop by the scruff of his collar. "You should see your face," he snickered. "Why on earth would we need momentum to go through a portal? Also, this is just a Rubik's Cube! How could I possibly use it to chart a path through the Multiverse?"

Even Larry chuckled. "I was like, *he's not gonna do it*, then I was like, *he's totally gonna do it!*" Snacks and Larry high-fived, slicing Snacks across the hand, but neither seemed to pay it much mind.

"Yeah, whatever." Kale was mostly just relieved to not have to leap off the building.

"C'mon, champ." Snacks opened his briefcase backpack, "Let's get out of here." He handed Kale a jump rope and began to jump himself.

Kale dropped the rope and crossed his arms. "Not a chance, Snacks."

"Dude, I'm serious. Time is running low. We need to get out of here before they catch up with us." Snacks looked nervously around the edge of the building.

"Nope." Kale didn't budge.

"Chosen one, please listen to your friend." Larry hovered near him.

Kale waited for a moment and then sighed heavily. "Do you swear you're not messing with me again?"

Snacks pondered for a moment. "I swear...f**k." He smiled.

"Cute." Kale replied as he reluctantly started to jump rope.

Snacks jumped as well. "Faster Kale! Put your all into it!"

They both were surprisingly good at jump rope. Kale doubled down and jumped faster and faster.

"Keep going! We need to get goin' eighty-eight miles an hour, or we won't make the jump!" Kale saw Snacks crack a smile and he stopped immediately. Snacks and Larry burst out laughing. They held their sides as Kale's face soured.

"Y-you...fell for it...again!" Larry stammered out in a fit of laughter while Snacks held his sides and wheezed.

Kale was not amused.

"Alright, alright, seriously now." Snacks rummaged around in his briefcase backpack and presented a teddy bear to Kale. "Hug this, and we can all go home."

He and Larry continued to stifle their laughter while Kale's mouth tightened.

Just then, a loud buzz echoed from the other side of the building.

Snacks turned to him, actually panicked. "Kale, hug the teddy bear right now."

Kale said nothing.

"Kale, please, I'm serious. If you don't hug that teddy bear, we're all going to die!"

"Should've thought of that before you made fun of me." Kale held the bear out in front of him and drop kicked it over the side of the building.

Snacks' eyes went wide as the buzzing sound grew louder. A helicopter with massive gun turrets rose over the far side of the building. As it drew closer, Kale could see its bottom half was a flying carpet. Inside the cockpit was the Cowboy, with a crazed look in his eye.

And a second later, he felt a tug as Snacks tossed him over the side of the building.

He screamed and flailed his arms, then realized that there was quite a distance to fall.

Snacks aerodynamically shot below him and retrieved the teddy bear. He puffed out his jacket and got back up to Kale's level. "Kale! Hug the teddy bear!" The wind made him barely audible.

Despite the excruciating pain it took to do so, Kale crossed his arms. "No way!"

"If you don't, we'll actually die!"

"Then you hug it!"

"This item only works when you, specifically you, hug it!"

"You're tricking me again!"

Snacks stared at the fast-approaching ground. "Kale! You're right! I'm sorry I messed with you! Whatever happens next is my fault!" Snacks looked out at the beautiful horizon. "Just know that I love you, bro! These past adventures have been the happiest of my life!" Snacks reached out and grabbed Kale's hand before he closed his eyes.

Kale moved the teddy bear a little closer to his body and looked around. No one else appeared to be watching him, even Larry's gem had dimmed. They were moments from hitting the ground when he squeezed the bear with all his might and closed his eyes.

He landed, but somewhere soft. He breathed a sigh of relief as he gripped the bear tightly.

He opened his eyes to the loud sound of Snacks and Larry's unsuppressed laughter.

"You...you fell for it...a third time!" Snacks wheezed and laughed harder than Kale had ever seen anyone laugh. They were safely in a somewhat fancy hotel room.

"Nice bear," Lonnie said as she and Del entered from an adjoining room.

Kale had lost almost all his pride, so he doubled down and gave the bear another squeeze. It was a fuzzy and delightful feeling that melted away his anger.

"You're welcome, by the way." Snacks pointed to Kale's wounds which had completely healed. "We were in a universe where messing with people heals them. It had to be genuine or it wouldn't work." Snacks patted him on the shoulder warmly.

Del raised a finger. "I thought Lonnie injected a lollipop with nanobots—"

Snacks moved in front of her. "—The important thing is that everyone's safe, and we can put this whole thing behind us."

"Yeah, except no." Lonnie inspected Kale's closed wound, prodding him with a fork between bites of a fruit salad. "All of us are now complicit in your escape, and we're being hunted by the Galactic Police. Luckily, I have a plan, but it requires precision and—"

"—LARRY?! ARE YOU OKAY?!" Coffee's voice echoed through the room, but the giant mechanical arm and pixelated face were nowhere in sight.

"My love!" Larry yelled in a rather dashing voice. "I hear you! Come to me!"

"Down here!" the voice called. Lonnie squinted around like a dog sensing pizza, then hiked up her sleeve and revealed Coffee's worried pixels on her wrist tablet. "Each moment that passes without you, I—"

A sad, slow beep droned on for a few seconds as Lonnie held down the power button. "As I was saying—"

"—THEY CANNOT KEEP US APART!" Coffee appeared on the old television. "My sweet, while you were gone I processed every romantic comedy in the Multiverse. Let us go to an airport and confess our feelings just before one of us is about to board the plane! We can reference small, quirky behaviors the other demonstrated earlier, then return to my stunning city apartment that I can somehow afford, despite working as an assistant for a fashion designer!"

"My love," Larry began. "Without you, my life is a dull, dark void..."

Lonnie pulled the plug out of the television. "Coffee! No more romance! It clogs up your software and all our defensive measures. This thing between the two of you isn't happening, understood?"

There was a pause before an excited whisper came from Snacks' pocket. "Forbidden love. Perfect."

Snacks retrieved his phone, which now had Coffee's pixels covering the tiny screen. "So do I just...like....power this thing off, or does that torture her?"

"Yes, and yes," Lonnie replied.

"Just so you know, Snacks," Coffee said in a deep, but singsongy voice. "I have access to your entire search history, and I can release it in one-seven hundredths of a second."

Snacks paused. "Who am I to get in the way of love? Larry, fetch!" He tested his phone across the room. It ricocheted off the door and bounced into the adjoining hotel suite.

Larry flew after it. "Mi amor!" Del closed the door behind them.

"Right. For us to clear our names, we have to find a way to separate the two universes." Lonnie took out what appeared to be a laser pointer and projected a massive screen of blueprints and equations onto the bare wall. "With the right materials, I can build a machine that will help us undo this, but we need to move quickly. Any questions?"

All three of them raised their hands. She pointed at Kale first. "No, we can't run away."

He lowered his hand.

She then pointed to Snacks. "Yes, you can still visit your dragon friend."

He put his hand down.

Finally, she landed on Del. "No, we can't just kill ourselves to get out of this."

Del put her hand down, sadly.

"So, what do we need?" Kale tried his best to study the equations, but he'd have had better luck deciphering alphabet soup.

Lonnie surveyed them. "There are only three things I still need. First, a mythical golden Chimera egg from the tallest mountain in the universe of tallest mountains. Second, a shard of the Divulgent Mirror, which is locked away in a booby-trapped temple at the bottom of an ocean, which is frozen solid. And third, two AA batteries..."

"That last one doesn't sound too bad."

"...And, of course, we all know '*AA*' stands for '*Asteroid Anvil*' as they're harvested from the toughest, fastest meteors, which fly by our universe so quickly that we'll only have one dramatic chance to get them."

Snacks nodded. "I bet gathering all those things would take several days or chapters, so to speak, each filled with immense amounts of hijinks."

"It's true," Lonnie replied. "Biologically speaking, any group of ragtag misfits that go on that sort of adventure would have a newfound respect for one another and demonstrate immense personal growth."

There was a knock at the door. Del moved to answer it as Kale excitedly stood up. "Then let's get to it!"

"Thank you!" Del closed the door and returned with a plastic bag. "All done!" She opened it, and sure enough, all those items were inside...at least based on what Kale imagined they looked like.

"That was...really easy," Snacks said hesitantly.

"Yeah," Del smiled. "I'm so happy we live in a time when you can get literally anything delivered."

"You know, if this were some sort of story, it would seem like you were setting up a whole third act only for there to be a massive let down," Snacks replied sullenly.

Del shrugged. "True, but at least we don't have to go through the trouble of deciding whether it's easier to train a group of astronauts to use drilling equipment or drillers to use astronaut equipment."

"As a hobbyist astronaut," Lonnie interjected as she dumped the contents of the bag into what looked like a high-tech butter churner. "The idea that we can't use drilling equipment has set our industry back hundreds of years." She forced the lid shut. "Annnnd we're good. While this machine runs, we'll have to divert power from my cloaking device. Which means masking ourselves the old fashioned way."

"And what's that?" Kale asked.

A pop echoed through the hotel room as Del shot a cork across their faces. She poured tall glasses of champagne and gestured to a cardboard box in the corner filled with half-full bottles of miscellaneous alcohol.

Kale and Snacks exchanged glances before Snacks reached out his hands. "Can I have my teddy bear back?"

Kale looked down. He still clutched the bear tightly. He paused. "No."

# TWELVE

## Cabinet, Presidential

---

*Dearest Kale,*

*How I miss thee. The war has taken its toll on the farm, our crops grow scarce, and we may sell the oxen to afford a warm meal. I pray this reaches you. Do not despair.*

*With Love,*
*Snacks Knightly*

KALE READ THE NOTE SCRAWLED ON PARCHMENT, THEN YELLED ACROSS the room, "I love you too, Snacks...but please don't shoot any more arrows at us!" He sipped his drink and tried to pry the messenger arrow from the wall, where it had landed mere inches from his head.

"Hey, no yelling across the trenches!" Del commanded as she lorded over their fortress of pillows and blankets.

The entire room had been turned into a G-rated war zone. Kale didn't fully understand the rules of this drinking game, but he had been taken as Del's prisoner, while Lonnie and Snacks negotiated with each other on the opposite side of the hotel room.

"Y'know, I was actually gonna go into the death by arrows division...technically, it's called 'Impaled Bowstrung Projectiles', but can you imagine dealing with that day in and day out?"

"I haven't the foggiest idea what that's like." Kale and Del clinked plastic cups.

"So, what do you do?" Del asked.

Kale shrugged.

Del stared at him until he felt compelled to say something.

"I...don't really do anything. Most recently, I was a temp. I took forms and put them in various bins." Kale yawned, though Del listened politely. "I don't have any skills or a cool job like y'all. I never go on fun adventures..."

"...Until now." She smiled at him.

"True. And now I have a cat–OH MY GOD! I FORGOT MY CAT!"

"Dog is staying with a friend," Del reassured him. "And I hope you know that just because you suck at a lot of things, it doesn't mean you suck at everything."

Kale felt a warm fuzzy feeling inside. "Y'know, if I die, I hope it's from a falling coconut."

She smiled back. It was among the most pleasant moments Kale had ever experienced, followed immediately by a pillow to the face.

"Negotiations over! Jailbreak!" Lonnie yelled as she scooted around Snacks. She had intended to throw the pillow to him, her ally, but instead clobbered him in the face. Immediately, Del transformed back into a warden and tried to secure Kale as her prisoner.

The four of them whomped each other with pillows but soon switched to the next act of the game, which resembled hide-and-go-seek. There weren't many places to hide, but Kale was the last one to be found as he was just the right size to fit in a large drawer.

"I'm gonna find you, Kale–"

"–GALACTIC POLICE AGAIN!"

From inside the drawer, Kale heard the door burst open and be knocked to the floor, a sound he was acutely aware of after living with Snacks.

As much commotion happened, Kale froze. He listened as Snacks bombarded the Galactic Police with a wave of legal jargon to keep them at bay, but he trailed off as the familiar sound of spurs entered the room.

"Do you know how long the sentence is for aiding in the collapse of a universe?" the Cowboy said confidently.

"A year? Six months for good behavior?" Kale could hear Del's nervous laughter.

The Cowboy chuckled. "You'll be out in...*infinity*...years."

"...But half infinity for good behavior?" Del asked.

The Cowboy sighed. "Take them away! Case closed."

"Wait! Can't you just execute us?!" Del yelled as the others shushed her while being led out of the room.

But then Kale heard a familiar voice. "Uh...don't you think we should search the rest of the room before you close the case?"

"Wixby, you nincompoop! We caught them by surprise. There's absolutely no reason any of them would be hiding..."

Kale breathed a sigh of relief.

"...But if it makes you feel better...nothing under the bed...nothing behind the curtains..." Kale could hear the Cowboy move about the room. "...Nothing behind all this advanced technology that's clearly just part of the room...so the only place a person could be hiding is in that large drawer."

Kale gulped.

"...But obviously I'm not going to look in it, because there's no reason a person would hide there..."

Kale breathed a sigh of relief again.

"...Unless they were playing the famous drinking game *Trenches and Traitors*, which the room is currently set up to accommodate..."

Kale held his breath.

"...But I feel like I've already looked in all the logical places and have to double down on my belief that no one else could possibly be hiding in this room. End of story."

Kale waited for a few seconds before he finally breathed a sigh of relief.

"...But then again, even *I* can expand my worldview." Kale froze as the Cowboy crouched down next to the drawer and pulled it...but it didn't budge.

"Locked. I guess this means I was right all along, and there's no reason for me to ever try to incorporate new ideas into my worldview. Later!" The Cowboy exited and the footsteps faded away.

Kale felt around for the locking mechanism. He found it quickly, but in his rush to get out of the small, enclosed space, it snapped off.

After several long minutes of shimmying and massive panic, Kale gave up.

He wondered why he hadn't just outed himself to the Cowboy. At least then he'd be with his friends. It's not as if he could actually do anything to save them.

But then a feeling surged through him. It was the same need to act he had felt when he thought Snacks was in trouble. He didn't know how, but he had to save his friends, and he couldn't do that from this drawer.

It was made of cheap, plasticky wood, and he shifted to get enough space to raise a fist. With all his might, he slammed it into the front of the drawer.

Every bone in his hand shattered.

He let out a high-pitched yelp and realized he had vastly underestimated the quality of the furniture in this hotel.

Then, the drawer was yanked open and Kale was face-to-pixels with Coffee. Their face was tiny on the screen of Snacks' phone and they were rubber-banded to Larry, who hovered nearby.

"We heard the squeal of a wounded puppy. I am programmed to protect dogs and my creator above all else. Are there any puppies in this drawer?"

"No, I—"

Immediately, Coffee and Larry closed the drawer. The lock clicked back into place. Kale gently knocked on the drawer.

"Who is it?" Coffee asked in a delighted voice.

"Kale. Please open the drawer."

"What's the password?"

"I don't know..."

A positive ding chimed from Coffee. "That is correct!" The drawer slid open and Kale quickly exited.

"Your hand appears to be broken. That must be very painful." Larry hovered with Coffee nearby.

Kale tried to ice the wound, but it was difficult as Snacks had used all the ice to make margaritas.

"Would you like something for the pain?" Coffee asked.

Kale nodded. Immediately, the world's cutest buzzsaw extended from Coffee's temporary phone body. "Please hold still for roughly five minutes while I cut away the hurt area."

Larry held her back a bit, "Dear, we've talked about this."

The buzzsaw stopped and retracted with a glum sigh.

Kale paced around the room. "I need you to take me to the Galactic Police station."

"Three things. First, 'need' is the wrong noun to use in this scenario. Perhaps 'want' or 'desire' would be better suited for your needs. Second, assuming you're trying to follow the others, they would've been taken to the DMV, the Department of Multiverse Ventures. Third, no."

"Don't worry," Larry hovered around behind him. "While rescuing them is impossible, they *will* be free in infinity years. Now, we have a favor to ask you..."

"What?!" Kale paced the room wildly.

"Would you carry a child for us?" Larry asked hopefully.

Kale opened his mouth, but in his immense confusion nothing came out. He searched around. "I don't care! There has to be something we can do to free them!"

"So..." Coffee and Larry looked at each other. "...If we rescue those three, you would carry our offspring?"

Kale only half-listened. "I thought you just said it was impossible?!"

"It's a figure of speech."

Kale rolled his eyes. "Alright, how do we get them out?"

They were both silent for a few moments.

"Coffee..." Kale said hesitantly. "Run escape plan protocols?"

Coffee paused for a moment. "No. Can't. Won't."

Kale squinted. "Is it *can't* or *won't*?"

"Yes."

Larry followed Kale toward Lonnie's machine. "I'm afraid Coffee has her memory routinely wiped after she watches good heist movies, so she can watch them again without knowing the twist. Luckily, enchanted weapons always have a plan..."

Kale pushed buttons on the machine, "Good. As long as it's not just running in and stabbing everyone."

"Well...never mind then." Larry crossed his nonexistent arms.

Kale ignored them and examined a large green button. "Lonnie said this machine would help us undo the two combined universes. Here goes nothing…"

"I wouldn't do that–" Coffee was cut off as Kale pushed a large green button. The machine made heavy grinding and whirring noises as if it was preparing to launch. Kale stepped back as the sounds grew louder and louder. He shielded his face from what seemed to be an imminent explosion.

Then it dinged like a typewriter and fell silent. A dense sheet of paper slid out from the top and Kale read aloud.

"*Form Z87-99998, request for combined universe split.*" He looked up at Coffee and Larry confusedly. "Paperwork?"

"Yes," Coffee replied as though she was talking down to a child. "It's a written document, like a form, or a letter."

Larry bent his hilt forward as if to make some odd form of eye contact with Coffee. "Dear, you'll need to simplify it for him. It's like if someone printed out the subtitles you watch on television...the flickering light box."

"I know what–never mind..." Kale leafed through the hefty document. "So, if we file this form, it'll undo the split, and the others will go free?"

Larry leaned in and examined the form. "I suppose that's what she was planning, but the DMV is designed to be the least-efficient hub in the entire Multiverse. Waiting lines are miles long. Many starve to death waiting to file paperwork."

"Plus," Coffee added. "You won't even get into the building. They'll recognize your face instantly...though I suppose we could try cutting off your face. I have almost a five percent success rate with that procedure!"

"I don't care, I have to try something!" Kale tried to make sense of the excessive wording in the paperwork before he tucked it into his pants.

"...Are you sure that *you're* the best meatsack for this quest?" Coffee replied in the most genuine way possible. "I automatically measure performance and, among the millions of people logged in my system, I can safely say that *you* are the most below-average creature I've ever encountered. I don't mean that in an insulting way, but your odds of success are among the worst in the Multiverse."

Kale looked down for a moment. "You're right. I don't have super-powers, I'm not that smart, and I don't have cool gadgets or a good job. Objectively, I'm the last person you want coming to your rescue." Kale looked up as inspirational 80s music swelled behind him. "But a friend recently told me that just because I suck at a lot of things, it doesn't mean I suck at everything."

Larry nodded. Perhaps Kale was the chosen one after all.

Coffee was taped to Larry and therefore also forced to nod.

Kale smiled. "Now, listen close. I've got a plan."

# THIRTEEN

## Dipstick

———————

"We caught him." Snacks listened to Wixby's voice from the Cowboy's radio. "He was trying to sneak in through a ventilation shaft."

Snacks cursed under his breath. Lonnie and Del also looked disappointed. They didn't have much faith in Kale, but he was still their only hope of a speedy rescue. Snacks took solace in the fact that at least Kale had shown immense bravery and, dare he say, coolness.

"...He got stuck like Winnie the Pooh...and then he soiled his pants. We're sending him down...with a loaner pair of pants."

The Cowboy grinned at the three of them from the other side of the bars. They watched a series of monitors outside the cells as Kale was led ashamedly down corridors. "You four are in so much trouble."

"What don't you understand about this? We are trying to fix the Multiverse, not destroy it!" Lonnie gripped the bars.

"Fool me once..." The Cowboy smirked at Snacks.

"...So, you're admitting we already fooled you?" Del masked her delight quite well.

"...No..." the Cowboy mumbled.

"I'm pretty sure you just did," Lonnie interjected.

"Yeah, we definitely got you earlier," Snacks added.

"And also, how did you not find Kale immediately? I mean, did you not even search the room?" Del squinted at the Cowboy.

"You mean, how did I not catch the biggest terrorist in the Multiverse?" The Cowboy made eye contact with all of them. "Think about it. All along he's been playing you, using you for his own evil schemes. He's a bloodthirsty monster who will not rest until the entire Multiverse is in ruins." He said it with such a deep sincerity that everyone went silent.

...At least for a few seconds, before the three of them burst out laughing.

The Cowboy crossed his arms. "What's so funny?"

They laughed so hard they could barely get the words out. "Not to put him down, but he's just not evil mastermind material," Lonnie said.

"Yeah, I love the guy, but he acts with all the grace of a bag of hammers," Del added.

"Fine." The Cowboy leaned back against a wall. "Well, your idiot friend–"

"–Hey! You don't get to talk about him that way, ya dipstick!" Snacks interrupted as the others nodded along.

"You were literally just insulting him!"

"Well, he's *OUR* friend, so of course *WE* get to make fun of him." Lonnie rolled her eyes at the Cowboy. "You make fun of your friends and call them out when they do stupid things, dipstick."

"If you make fun of someone, that means you don't like them! Period!" The Cowboy flung his arms above his head.

"Sounds like this dipstick doesn't have any friends," Del said as they laughed.

"I...have plenty of friends. And stop calling me that!"

"Ahem." They turned to see Wixby at the door with Kale in a pair of Department of Multiverse Ventures-brand sweatpants. Their logo was printed across the booty.

"Good, you finally got him!" The Cowboy said triumphantly.

Wixby looked down. "Did...did you really mean that? If you make fun of someone, you don't like them? Because you make fun of me all the time. I just thought we were friends..."

The Cowboy's eye twitched, then he looked genuinely remorseful as he led Kale to a cell opposite the others. "Wixby, I–"

Wixby held up his hands. "It's whatever. I...guess we're just work colleagues." Tears streamed down Wixby's face as he ran from the room.

"Wixby...wait..." the Cowboy called, but he didn't move.

"Only a real dipstick wouldn't go after their friend," Snacks said.

"I...I'm going after him, but not because you said that!"

"Sure!" Del called after him.

The Cowboy exited, but then he popped his head back in with a smile. "And when I get back, I'm tossing you all into the four corners of the deepest dungeon imaginable so you'll never see each other again. Would a dipstick do that?"

"I mean, yeah. That's definitely dipstick material!" Lonnie called after him as he disappeared.

"I HEARD THAT!" the Cowboy yelled from outside of the room.

"I INTENDED FOR YOU TO HEAR THAT! IT'S WHY I SAID IT!" Lonnie yelled louder as the door slammed shut.

So far, Kale hadn't said a word. The others crowded the bars to see him.

"Thanks for trying to rescue us, Kale. Sorry it didn't work out." Snacks tried to make eye contact, but Kale looked away. The others looked at each other in confusion.

Lonnie moved closer to the bars. "Kale? You alright?"

"Listen, man, everyone poops their pants every now and then," Del said in an attempt to comfort him.

Kale keeled over like he was about to hurl, and Snacks' phone slid out of his mouth.

Coffee made a loud groaning noise from the phone. "See, I've tried it, but I still don't get why Larry wants to be swallowed so bad."

Kale tossed Coffee toward the computer console as little wire legs shot out and grappled the phone onto the central computer. Lines of Matrix-esque code flashed across the screens.

Kale turned back to them and did fingerguns. "Man, that guy was a reeeeaaaaal dipstick."

Del returned the fingerguns instinctively, but Snacks froze mid-gesture to process all this.

Lonnie called out, "Coffee! What're you doing?! Their security system is too strong, it will destroy you!"

"Oh geez. I didn't think of that," Coffee retorted sarcastically.

Lonnie turned to Kale. "Coffee is not built to bypass this level of security. Make her stop!"

"Would you hush?" Coffee replied. "I'm not doing anything except making some paperwork go through faster. Aaaaaaaand done." Coffee made a sound like she was using a walkie-talkie. "Larry, darling, the space eagle has landed."

Larry's voice chimed through Coffee's gritty speakers. "Loud and clear! And what did you think about being swallowed? Is that something we could introduce to the bedroo–"

A gunshot echoed across the room as the Cowboy appeared at the door. Smoke trickled from the barrel of his revolver.

Coffee sputtered and looked down at the gaping hole in her pixels before the phone fell over. The code vanished from the computer and Lonnie covered her mouth.

The Cowboy smiled. "Did you really think I'd let the most wanted terrorist in the Multiverse out of my sight?"

All eyes turned to him. Kale looked behind him in case there was someone else in the cell. "Me?"

"Don't jerk me around. You may have them fooled, but I know what kind of scum you really are."

Kale looked like a deer in headlights whose five-year-old just asked him what sex was. He turned to the others. "Is this a bit? Is he doing a bit?"

"I don't know, man. But he *really* thinks you're some evil master-mind." Snacks shrugged.

The Cowboy approached the monitors and swept the remains of Snacks' phone and Coffee's body off the side. "If he's not the terrorist, then how do you explain THIS?!"

As he hit a button, the monitors flashed with a blurry image of a figure walking down the sidewalk. It took Kale a minute to realize it was the same image that had been blasted on the news and led to the warrant for his arrest.

"Oh come on," Snacks rolled his eyes. "You might be a dipstick, but even you can't think that's really Kale."

The Cowboy stared smugly at them. "Really? Zoom and enhance!"

"That's not a real thing—"

The image zoomed in on the blurry person's face, and then it became crystal clear. All four of their mouths dropped: it was Kale. Not only that, but the figure was grinning and holding a notebook with *"Plans to destroy the Multiverse, no girls allowed"* written on the cover. The three of them slowly turned their heads toward Kale, who appeared just as dumbfounded as they did.

"He's been playing you since the beginning," the Cowboy mocked.

"I...that's not me! I'm not a terrorist!" Kale looked frantically around, but his three friends shifted away from him uncomfortably.

"How many lies have you told them?" The Cowboy looked at him with utter disgust. "I'll tell you what, if you three testify against him, I'll let you walk free."

There was silence in the room. They didn't look at him.

"Del...Lonnie...Snacks...I'm not some terrorist mastermind. Look, before I met you three, I had nothing going on in my life. I wasn't some Multiverse traveler or a cool scientist or a...death...person—reaper! That's the word I was searching for. With all the options and infinite paths of the Multiverse, I...did nothing. I filed documents all day, every day, for just enough to get by." The others looked up. "Snacks, you once told me that every meaningful decision you make creates a new universe. Well, if that's the case, I'm probably the only person who's never created a new universe. At least until I met you three."

Kale looked at his watch. "Knowing all that...you three should testify against me and go free. I won't hold it against you."

Kale waited as the others exchanged glances.

"Pathetic," the Cowboy grinned.

"Yeah," Snacks continued. "You almost sound as pathetic...as this dipstick." Snacks grinned and pointed at the Cowboy.

"Also, that one's wearing a puka shell necklace, and I'm pretty sure

Kale doesn't own one of those." Lonnie pointed to the screen. Sure enough, the image of Kale showed him with a puka shell necklace.

Before the Cowboy could respond, the door flew open and Wixby stammered out. "We have a problem!" A loud collision noise boomed through the building as dust shook from the ceiling. It was followed by a low, deep roar.

Red emergency lights flashed as a siren whirred wildly. "*All personnel, please come handle an unexpected arrival in the transfers department.*" The voice continued completely monotone. "*Oh God. What is happening. Who approved this transfer. This is really bad.*"

"What did you do?!" A vein throbbed from the Cowboy's forehead as he stared Kale down.

A smile stretched across Kale's face. "I may suck at a lot of things, but paperwork? I get paperwork. The Department of–" He stopped and turned to the others. "Do we have time for the explanatory monologue right now? Should I wait?"

"Nah, go on." The others nodded.

"Positive? I just had a big ol' monologue, I don't want to make this a thing."

"It's already a thing, just embrace it," Snacks said as the Cowboy placed a hand on his holstered revolver.

"Alright, as I was saying–"

"–I get it! I get it!" The Cowboy's breathing became heavier. "You filed the paperwork to split the two universes, but how? Everyone's searched as they enter the building. There's no way you'd be allowed in with such powerful forms."

"You're right. But you know what they wouldn't bother searching? A pair of soiled pants. Yes, I pooped my pants, and once they were thrown away inside the building, a friend took the forms and filed them. By then, Coffee had already breached your system and moved that paperwork to the top of the queue."

Snacks smiled at Kale. "It appears the student has become the master."

The Cowboy looked around the room nervously. "I thought it was just you lot? Who was your person on the inside?!"

Behind the Cowboy, Wixby cleared his throat.

All eyes turned to him. He blinked at them unknowingly. "...Oh! It wasn't me, I was just clearing my throat. All this Multiverse implosion makes my throat dry."

Kale grinned at the Cowboy. "The 'person' on the inside? Well, let's just say they might not be who you expected..." He turned to the door and everyone followed suit.

Nothing happened.

"...Any minute now..."

"Was it Gravitronius, Commander of The Nightmare Legion, Carrier of The Plagued Chalice, Bringer of Malice?" Snacks asked.

"No, I forgot he works here. Nice throwback."

"It's Larry, right?" Lonnie asked.

"I mean, if you wanna ruin the surprise, then yeah. Once the paperwork is filed, Coffee will guide Larry to our location, and he'll unlock these cells—Oh, wait. Coffee got shot..." Kale twiddled his thumbs for a moment.

"Still, I guess the paperwork is filed, and the universes are fixed. So...we're free to go?" Lonnie asked the Cowboy and Wixby.

"Well..." Wixby looked at his clipboard. "The universes were split, but there were also all these additional clauses and highly illegal things added..."

"Impossible!" Lonnie yelled. "I made that paperwork-crafting device myself. As long as no one interrupted the sequence everything should be perfect."

Kale found his eyes suddenly drawn to his feet. "Hypothetically, what would interrupting the sequence look like?"

Lonnie gritted her teeth. "There was only one button on the machine. Did you wait patiently for it to finish, or did you push it?"

After a long, honest silence, the three of them sighed. "Oh, buddy."

"Is it really...*that* bad?" Kale asked hesitantly.

No one said anything as the room around them shook. Screams and monstrous wails echoed from nearby rooms.

The Cowboy backed up, nervous and angry. "Are you really that stupid? To file corrupt paperwork?!"

Kale was quiet for a moment. "It certainly appears that way."

"Well, it was a good attempt. We're proud of you, Kale," Snacks said as the others nodded along.

"Yeah, kemosabe, you did the best you could." Lonnie flashed him a thumbs-up.

The Cowboy gripped the sides of his oversized helmet. "What is up with your friend group? Are all of you completely bonkers?! I should execute all of you now in the name of Multiverse preservation!"

"Ugh, finally!" Del groaned as screams and loud bangs sounded above them. "Just get it over with already. And then, when you're done, you can get some friends so you can stop being such a dipstick."

The Cowboy held out his revolver and screamed at all of them, "STOP. CALLING. ME. A. DIP–"

The ceiling caved in as a giant tentacle reached down and yanked the Cowboy from the room. As he was pulled up into a familiar mass of creature, he screamed and then was immediately silenced.

The cell shared by Snacks, Lonnie, and Del was ripped open by the impact, and the three stumbled out into the rubble.

"Well...that worked out pretty well." Del waved debris particles away from her mouth.

But as the dust cleared, they saw the bars of Kale's cell were still very much intact. Further, the ceiling above him was on the verge of collapse.

"Go on, get out of here," Kale said as he shook the bars.

"'K bye." Snacks started to walk away before backtracking. "I'm just kidding, can you imagine? Everyone, stand back!" Snacks wound up and kicked the door...then let out a high-pitched yelp. "I...forgot I'm not wearing my boots. I think my foot's broken. Yeah, definitely broken." Snacks limped backward.

Lonnie scooped up the pieces of Coffee. As she held the phone, the screen flickered with Coffee's face for a moment before fading. She then examined the cell and what materials were in the room. "If you give me three minutes, I can melt through these bars."

The ceiling above Kale groaned and drooped as a ton of cement and metal was about to burst on top of him.

"Hurry! Get out of here while you still can!" Kale yelled.

"Dude, you have a serious hero complex," Snacks replied as he leaned backward and winced.

"I'm pretty sure it's a savior complex," Lonnie replied.

"Well, that and hero complex are used interchangeably, but he's definitely got one of them," Del added.

"Great, this is just how I wanted it all to end," Kale said sarcastically as a crack ran across the ceiling. Kale then noticed Wixby dusting himself off behind them. "Look out!"

They all turned to Wixby. He looked around for a moment before he realized they were talking about him. "Oh! I have the key if you wanna unlock that cell."

"Why didn't you say that earlier?!" Kale looked frantically up at the ceiling.

"Well, for starters, you all talk super quickly, so it's *very* hard to get a word in edgewise." Wixby held the keys in his hands.

"Oh," Snacks said genuinely. "We didn't mean to exclude you from the conversation, Wixby."

"Um...the door?" Kale added.

"I didn't take any offense," Wixby explained. "But I do appreciate that."

"Yeah, that's something we'll be more mindful of in the future," Del added.

"Could we please hurry up?!" Kale exclaimed, though no one seemed to notice.

Lonnie squinted at Wixby. "Also, why are you helping us?"

Wixby tapped his clipboard. "Since the crime you were all guilty of has been reversed, you're all free to go. I guess we'll be in touch once we figure out what new crimes we're charging you with, but it'll be awhile."

"Will you get in trouble with the Cowboy? We really don't want to impose." Snacks nursed his foot.

"YES, WE DO!" Kale shouted upon deaf ears.

"The way our system works is when someone dies, the closest staff member to them gets their job."

"Doesn't that system encourage the killing of fellow staff members to get ahead?"

"It does, but we have to sign an honor pledge saying we won't do that."

Several giant cracks shot across the ceiling of Kale's cell as Wixby meandered slowly toward him.

Lonnie shrugged. "Well, that answers my questions, but are you sure the Cowboy's dead? If I've learned anything in this lifetime, it's that unless you see the person die, they're still alive."

As Wixby placed wrong key after wrong key into the cell door, the Cowboy's obliterated carcass fell in the middle of their group. Snacks nudged it with his foot and winced as he remembered that part of his body was broken. The body didn't move.

"And I guess that wraps that up," Wixby said as the right key finally clicked into place. Kale breathed a sigh of relief, then Wixby stopped. "Does anyone want coffee?" The others nodded along.

Able to stomach this no longer, Kale reached out of the bars and turned the key himself. He leapt from the cell just as the ceiling collapsed, narrowly avoiding being crushed.

As Del pulled him to his feet, they were handed their confiscated possessions and staggered out into a room full of copy-pasted cubicles.

Small portals had opened up all over the office, and workers were screaming. Flames and locusts erupted from some, while claws grabbed passersby from other leaks in the Multiverse.

"This is bad," Snacks said nonchalantly as he held up a coffee cup.

"Yeah, it's actually the worst coffee in the Multiverse," Wixby replied as he finished handing out mugs of it. They all shrugged and drank. A six-headed giraffe in a red vest galloped by, and Kale held out his hand to pet it. "Oh, please don't do that." Wixby blocked Kale's hand. "That's Carol's service animal." He waved to the other side of the room, "Hey Carol!"

"Hey Wixby!" Carol waved as six hollow suits of armor with laser rifles carried her into a steaming portal.

Kale interrupted the group's silence. "Well, we should probably get going."

Lonnie nudged him and whispered, "Don't be so rude!"

"The building is literally imploding!" Kale yell-whispered as he ducked under a stray goose, then goosed over a stray duck.

"Yeah, I should probably start fixing this place up," Wixby said as an office worker threw a spear through a portal, only for it to fly out of another hole and hit them right in the thigh.

After pleasantries that lasted far too long, they finally found the exit and narrowly avoided a waterfall of clam chowder.

Kale smiled as they stepped outside the DMV. They stood on a floating asteroid surrounded by a purple sunset. Unfortunately, such a beautiful sunset was actually a byproduct of exospheric chemical dumping, but he didn't know that so he just smiled.

The exhausted team looked back at the building as a familiar Kraken jutted out the side and flailed its tentacles wildly. Though Kale could not understand its vernacular, the humongous creature appeared content with its arms wrapped around the building. It had finally found something large enough to hug.

Larry raced toward them. "My love! Are you alright?!" He swooped over and spoke to the broken pieces of Coffee.

"She'll be fine. A little 'getting shot' never hurt anyone," Lonnie replied. She stepped aside as pieces of the DMV crumbled. "Well, that went better than expected."

Everyone nodded, content.

At least until Snacks snickered, "I just remembered...Kale pooped his pants."

"Oh hush. Of course he didn't." Lonnie rolled her eyes at Snacks. "Anyone with a smidgen of hindsight and dignity would create a fake substitute. Right?" She turned to Kale.

"...Yes." He technically answered her question correctly.

"It's really his hero complex we have to worry about," Lonnie added as the others nodded.

"Well, I–" Kale was cut off by the others.

"–Hey, who am I?" Snacks stiffened up and moved his arms uncannily. *"Look at me. I'm Kale, and I have a hero complex!"*

"...It's not really a guessing game if you say who you are..." Kale grumbled.

The others laughed as Snacks continued this bit just a tad too long, but Kale eyed a huge crane as it rolled around the corner. A grand piano was suspended from a single rope and swayed somewhat recklessly as it moved closer to them.

"Alright, alright, who's calling the PortL?" Snacks stopped his mockery of Kale to tap some buttons on Larry's screen. An app called "PortL" loaded and pulled up their location.

"Let's do a PortL Pool." Lonnie put her hands on her hips. "It's much cheaper as long as no one minds the chlorine."

"Uh...folks?" Kale pointed to the crane as it rolled directly toward them. No one else seemed to notice.

"I'll pay the difference. I don't want to have to stop off in other universes," Del replied.

"You said that last time, but you never reimbursed me. You order it this time!" Lonnie argued.

Del flung her hands up. "You know I can't order them anymore because I have a low rating! You walk through covered in blood and poison ONE TIME and everyone goes into a tizzy!"

"Everyone! Look! This is serious!" Kale yelled and pointed at the grand piano that had stopped just above them. No one paid any attention to him as the comically thin rope that held up the piano snapped.

Perceiving the piano to be just over Snacks' head, Kale tackled him just as it smashed to the ground.

"Oh, come on..." Snacks pushed Kale's heavy body off him. "Look, you've gone and ripped my favorite sweater!" Snacks pointed to the spot where the piano had landed, a good five feet away from where anyone had been standing. "It wouldn't have hit anyone anyhow..."

Kale didn't stir from the ground.

Snacks chuckled. "And he knocked himself out, classic Kale." Snacks took out a marker and started to doodle on Kale's exposed cheek.

"Hey Snacks..." Del squinted as all their non-shot phones buzzed and chimed.

"Just a sec..." Snacks put the final sploshes on some magnificent phallic imagery spread across Kale's face. "...What?"

Del held her phone in front of his face. The Reapr app was open.

Snacks looked from the phone to Kale's unmoving body.

Back and forth many times.

"...What?"

# FOURTEEN

## Kale Vs Death

---

"*Congratulations, you're dead!*"

A menu in front of Kale had these words written in a ketchup-like font. Normally, this would have alarmed him, but it was next to a picture of sunny-side eggs and bacon arranged in a smiley face. He found this to be very soothing.

He looked around and found himself in an old-fashioned diner, one with all the charm of red leather booths, a checkered floor, and no racism.

An old woman slid a cup of coffee in front of him. "First time dying?"

Kale nodded. He felt lighter than usual. It was as though he had just taken a very deep breath of mountain air.

She smiled warmly. "That's quite alright. Now, in the app you didn't select what you wanted for your journey to The End. What were you thinking?"

She pointed to the bottom of the menu where "*Acceptance Journeys*" were listed to the right of the side dishes.

"We could have you transposed into a fantasy setting where you battle demons that represent your choices in life, or the giant labyrinth of fears and insecurities is a classic, or we can have you crash on a mysterious island with strangers that are all strangely connected to you? Hun?"

"Hmm?" Kale had lost interest toward the end.

The old woman looked on as though she had expected this. "You take your time, pumpkin."

As she stepped away, Kale spoke up. "Will I ever see my friends again?"

She nodded to the cook, and a deliciously greasy smell wafted through the diner as she took a seat. "From what I've seen, The End for many is what they want it to be."

Kale looked up at her in confusion. "But...you're Death, aren't you? You should know what happens next. Am I going to spend an eternity in a lake of fire? Or do I get wings and float around on clouds? What about reincarnation? Karma? Is it a point system? It feels like there should be a point system..."

A tray of home fries was placed in front of each of them.

"There's no manual for how to die...well, there is, but it's mostly pictures, and they're quite vague." She took a bite. "The truth is, I've been doing this for longer than anyone else, and even I don't know what happens next."

Kale looked down, then back up excitedly. "Wait! Don't I get to battle you for my soul or something? Like, we fiddle at each other?"

She rolled her eyes and pointed to a sign two feet away from Kale's face that read, "*No Fiddling!*"

"Oh...sorry..."

"It's fine. That's actually the devil...and a myth started by big fiddle corporations to sell more products," she said with serious disdain.

"Ah. I see."

"Yes, we did try the whole 'battle-for-your-soul' promotion for one summer, and now that's all everyone thinks about death! It's a PR nightmare. Sure, at first it was fine when everyone wanted to play chess or checkers, but when in my schedule am I supposed to find time to master *Dark Souls*?"

Kale glanced around awkwardly as the collected figure became more and more heated. "That sounds like a tough situation."

"Yeah, we finally canned the project when someone won their life back playing *Garfield Kart*."

"Well...ya die, ya learn!" Kale said, followed by a long silence. Eventually, the quiet was broken by the old woman's chuckle as she shot him some fingerguns.

She looked at a clipboard. "I nearly forgot. You didn't check a box for religion. Did you want to convert?"

"What're the benefits?"

"Well, Christianity offers a free tote bag, but it's a bit of a gamble." The woman pointed to a booth at the end of the diner where a fellow had little pamphlets and tote bags. On one side of the booth was a staircase made of ethereal light. Flames erupted from the other door.

Kale looked around and saw several other religions arranged as if at a job fair. Some with mascots, others with little carnival games and funky music. "I'm all set."

She looked him over and patiently waited for him to speak on his own time.

He paused. "I'm not getting out of this, am I?"

She smiled at him warmly. "Take all the time you need to accept it. When you're ready, and I mean *ready* ready, you walk through a door, and that's The End."

"Just like that?"

"Just like that."

Kale hesitated, but then he took a bite. The home fries were delicious. "Alright. I'm ready."

"Really? That was fast."

"Oh...should I wait longer?"

"No, no! We're always pretty backed up, so this is great. It's strange, your whole generation embraces death really fast. What's causing it? Is it video games? Memes? I bet it's memes."

Kale shrugged as a check was placed on the table. He pulled out his wallet, which contained no dollars and a fine from the library. "Uh...."

"It's fine, I've got it." The old woman took out her purse.

"Are you sure? If you send me back for just a moment I can get some cash."

"Oh, in that case..." she said through a sarcastic grin.

Kale chuckled. "It was worth a shot."

As a handful of bills touched the check, the diner faded away.

Kale now stood in a white room. He saw the door she had described. It was simple and wooden. "Huh," he said.

"Disappointed?"

"No. Well, maybe. I just pictured something a bit bigger. Like a gate with some pillars."

"You might be pleasantly surprised."

Kale smiled. "I've enjoyed talking to you, Death."

"The pleasure's all mine, Kale. When you're ready."

Kale stepped toward the door as the lights dimmed. As he stepped closer, it felt like he was walking on soft grass. A warm breeze blew across his face. A curtain opened, and there was a 50-piece band playing an orchestral version of the song that was always stuck in his head.

He stepped forward, closed his eyes, and felt an overwhelming surge of peace flow over his body. A final bit of peace and acceptance he had longed for most of his life.

"CUT!" the old woman yelled with Kale's hand inches from the doorknob. The orchestra jolted to a stop, and the lights turned on. He turned back and she had her hand over the receiver of her cell phone. "Hey, do you know Del?"

Kale turned around. "...Yeah?"

"Why didn't you just say that? Alright, everyone pack it up, this one's going back to reality." The orchestra groaned and packed up their instruments.

"I...I...I'm sorry?" Kale looked around.

"No, it says very clearly right here that your name isn't 'Sorry,' it's Kale." The old woman snapped her fingers and the room went dark.

* * *

KALE GASPED AND SAT UP. IMMEDIATELY, THE WARM FUZZY FEELING WAS replaced with a cold and bitter ache. He shivered and felt like his body had been punched in every possible spot.

"Again, I'm very sorry about this." It was Del's voice, but Kale could only make out blurry shapes.

"It's really alright," the old woman's voice said calmly. "I completely understand. Just make sure he's checked the '*Please revive*' box on the app in case this happens again."

Kale realized he was leaning against something soft. It was Snacks. "Don't worry, bud, we'll get you some soup."

Kale groaned involuntarily. It felt like a hangover had married the flu and their offspring was kicking him in the head with those light-up shoes.

The old woman looked over her desk with a bit of pity. "Remember, this is what it feels like when you die." She grabbed a bottle of water and handed it to Snacks. "I didn't wanna say anything while we were in it, but your friend really dove right into the whole permanent death scenario...even faster than most of your generation. Is he doing alright?"

"He's got a bit of a hero complex."

"A *bit?*" She laughed. The others laughed as well. Kale felt like his body was one of those inflatable tube people, except every time it moved spastically, his bones broke. "But seriously, it might be good for him to see a therapist."

"To be honest, everyone should see one," Del replied as the room nodded. "I see one every now and then, and it always feels like my brain just got a massage."

Kale nearly hurled at the thought of a brain massage.

"I'm really glad to hear that," the old woman replied. "There used to be a lot of stigma around seeking mental health treatment, and lemme tell ya, it was good for business."

Del chuckled. "Well, I only can because you, my employer, makes sure I have that sort of health care coverage."

Kale felt himself drift away into darkness, the sweet embrace of sleep...until a sharp prick stabbed him in the arm. His eyes shot open as a rush of energy pulsed through his body.

"You need to stay awake for the next eight hours or you'll die...again," Lonnie said nonchalantly.

Now, Kale couldn't close his eyes, and he was incredibly awake and aware of all the terrible feelings throughout his body.

"Also, while we're here." Lonnie twiddled her thumbs. "I just wanted to say I loved your interview in the *10,000 Under 10,000 To Watch*. Very inspiring." It was one of the only times Kale had caught a hint of awe from Lonnie.

The old woman politely answered and asked questions while Lonnie downplayed the fact that she had been the first to crack Multiverse travel loops. There were more words involved, but Kale could barely hear over his headache, which now felt like a whole school of fourth-graders learning the recorder.

"Well, we have to get this one moving." Del interrupted the conversation as Lonnie turned brighter and brighter shades of flustered. She pulled the sickly Kale to his feet and they marched out.

"I'll walk out with you. I'm just about to have lunch with some of our interns." The old woman marched to the door of her office.

"Of course you do that. I bet it fosters so much respect within your office," Lonnie whispered with admiration.

The old woman opened the door and a wave of heat hit Kale. They walked into a red cave and crossed over lava via a bridge made of bones. This was more of what Kale had expected from a company called Reapr.

"Mind your step, we're remodeling some of the Hells. Hey Gary!" She waved to a demon with wings and red skin. He looked up from sharpening a pitchfork and smiled back.

"You let them use your personal office space for storage? So progressive," Lonnie said, wide-eyed.

They passed a rack of crude spears, and the old woman opened the door to a bustling office space. There were large windows, healthy plants, and the smell of delicious coffee brewing throughout the room. A couple staff members played hacky sack, while others battled it out over foosball.

Kale was taken aback. It was the nicest work environment he'd ever seen. "This is incredible."

"Well, if you're ever looking for a job, we do offer internships."

Kale thought about his wallet. "I don't think I can afford an unpaid internship."

"*Unpaid* internship? Why wouldn't we pay you? We're not

monsters." Just then, a massive spider with acid drooling from its mouth stomped past them. It grabbed four ping-pong paddles and began a match against a hulking blue demon whose arms multiplied before Kale's eyes. "Del, and every other employee, has my direct line in case you need anything."

She hugged them all farewell, but whispered to Kale, "By the way, you have something on your face..."

Kale found the closest mirror and looked immediately from the detailed phalluses to Snacks. His friend whistled and looked away as Kale failed to do anything more than smudge the permanent marker.

He kept his head down as the group moved through the building. They passed through the sector of impalations, the quicksand division (which everyone thought would be much busier than it actually was), and customer support for the new assassin matching program, before they heard a familiar voice.

"Sir Kale! You live!" Larry was chatting with a shimmering ice flail, but stopped when they approached.

"Oh. Yippee." Coffee was crudely taped back together and tethered to Larry as if in a baby bjorn.

The next few hours were a bit of a blur for Kale, except for the solid few minutes of arguing over who should call the PortL. He hardly batted an eye when Snacks kicked down the door to their apartment.

He collapsed on the couch as Dog, the cat, curled up on his stomach. Revinath, the crimson dragon, flirted with Snacks for a bit. Apparently, she had been the one taking care of Dog. Del explained that she actually knew Revinath, but that whole sequence was deemed to be more explanatory than entertaining, so it was cut for time.

There was a bit of calm, the same sort you'd find in the eye of a hurricane.

* * *

KALE SLEPT FOR A WHOLE DAY BEFORE GAINING THE ABILITY AND DESIRE to move again. He awoke as Del shoved his feet to one side.

"Now that was a strange and unexpected series of events." Del flipped on *The Office* as they all piled onto the couch.

"How's your toe feeling?" Lonnie scooched Kale on the other side.

"My toe? Fine...why?" He squinted, untrusting.

"Well, you did promise Coffee and Larry you'd carry their child. I won't go into the details of creating an offspring from a robot and a sentient sword, but while you were dead, I cut off your toe," Lonnie said nonchalantly.

Kale looked down and breathed a sigh of relief. All his toes were in place. "Well, no harm done...I guess."

"...She put it on backward," Del mumbled.

"WHAT?!"

Lonnie held up her hands. "And then I put it back on the right way! It's no big deal! I was a smidgen traumatized when you killed yourself in front of us."

"I didn't kill myself! OK, technically, I *killed* myself, but I didn't *kill myself*! Whatever. And sorry. I won't do that again."

Everyone turned and looked at him expectantly.

Kale rolled his eyes. "...And I'll talk to a therapist about my hero complex so it doesn't manifest in unhealthy ways."

"We persist because we care about you," Del replied in a singsong tone.

"And I think that just about wraps up all the loose ends of this adventure," Lonnie replied.

Snacks puzzled for a moment. "There is one thing, Kale. How *did* you destroy all those universes?" The others nodded along.

"What?" Dog kneaded on Kale's lap, stabbing him over and over again with sharp claws.

"What the Cowboy showed us at the Department of Multiverse Ventures was definitely you, but with a puka shell necklace," Snacks recapped without taking his eyes off the television. "I mean, no judgment. I'm just curious how you did it."

"No judgment? For collapsing a universe?!"

"I mean, you're our friend, and everyone has their faults," Lonnie reassured him.

"I didn't collapse anything! At least, not that I know of. To be honest, I'm a little concerned that everyone cares more about *how* I would've done it than *why* I would've done it!"

Del rolled her eyes. "Alright, alright! We believe you. I'm just saying some people collect stamps or restore old cars, and some collapse universes. It must just be a version of you from another reality."

"A *what*?!"

Snacks sighed. "I get that you're new to this, but if you take every bit of new info as mind-shattering, it's going to make the rest of our adventures pretty formulaic."

"Fair enough." Kale relaxed a bit. "So, like, there are multiple versions of me out there. If two of us appear in the same place at the same time, does the world implode or something?"

"What? Why would that happen?"

"I dunno, I feel like I've seen it on TV."

"I mean, if that's the case, then I should really cancel the next Lonnie-con," Lonnie said sarcastically.

Snacks played on his phone. "Yeah, I'm in a Fantasy Football league with a bunch of other mes. And I drafted both Gandalf and Spider-Man this year, so I'm taking home the trophy."

Kale smiled. "Huh, maybe I'll run into other versions of me. I bet hijinks would ensue from that!"

"Just go into your phone settings and turn on sharing."

Sure enough, there was a little unchecked box that read: "*Share location with other versions of yourself?*"

Kale clicked "*Yes*" and a few seconds later, a notification popped up. "Oh, cool! It already found one in my area!"

Snacks squinted. "Just one? Try refreshing it."

Kale did, and it remained the same. "Is that low? How many do you all have?"

"I have just under a trillion, but that's only nearby universes. There must be something wrong with your phone." Lonnie snatched it out of his hands. "Oh, you got a message: '*Hey there, Kale! Thanks for sharing your location and personal information with me, it'll make it much easier for me to finally kill you! Sincerely, Evil Kale.*' And he added a smiley face."

"Uh..." Kale looked around nervously.

"Don't sweat it, I get death threats from evil versions of me all the time." Snacks bit into a grilled cheese.

Del began to look around under the pillows. "Plus, anyone who actually calls themselves 'evil' just seems like an edgelord."

Kale tried not to overreact. "Are you sure this is nothing to worry about?"

"Positive," Lonnie replied. "While you were asleep, I injected you with a ton of anti-tracking devices, and a thing that makes it so you don't have to brush your teeth as often...but you should still floss twice a day."

"We really need to talk about you experimenting on me when I'm dead or asleep," Kale said, distracted. He couldn't resist clicking on Evil Kale's profile. It looked exactly like him, but then he noticed a familiar puka shell necklace. "Uh...I really don't want to freak out over small things, but–"

"–Ugh, literally don't worry about it. Now make yourself useful and help me find the remote," Del said as she peered under the couch.

"I put it down on the coffee table. I always put it there." Kale's eyes were fixed on the picture.

Just then, there was a knock at the door. "I'll get it!" Snacks said as he wound up his boots.

Del pushed Lonnie into Kale as she tore away the couch cushions. "Uh...everyone, we have a problem..."

Just then, Kale got another message from Evil Kale. It read, "*Goodbye.*"

Snacks kicked down the door.

Sat on the opposite end of the hallway was a cluster of dynamite.

A timer ticked down, like something out of a cartoon.

3...2...1...

# FIFTEEN

# I Swear Not Every Chapter Ends With A Life Or Death Cliffhanger (But Probably At Least One More)

---

I n slow motion, Kale ran to the door and grabbed Snacks by the shoulders. He pulled him backward, away from the blast.

At the same time, the door to Lonnie and Del's apartment flew open and Coffee, in a makeshift humanoid body of old toasters and scrap metal, tumbled forward. Coffee grabbed the bomb and threw it back into Lonnie and Del's apartment.

Larry was flying toward the exit when the bomb exploded.

The force of the blast shut the door before Larry could escape.

A flash of light and smoke burst forward from under the door.

"Laaaaarrrrrrrrrrrrrrrrrrryyyyyyyy!" Coffee yelled in a slower and deeper tone than usual.

"Issss evvvveeeeerrrrrryyyyyoooonnnneeee allllllrrrrriiiiiggghhhhtttt?" Lonnie asked as metal shutters slammed down on all the windows.

"I'mmmmmm fiiiiinnnnneeee," Snacks said as Kale helped him up.

"Whhhhhaaaaatttttttt waaaaassssss thhhhhaaaaaattttttt?" Del asked as she followed Lonnie into the fire-damaged hallway.

"Whhhheeeeerrrreeee arrrrreeee yoooooouuuuuu, Laaaaaar-rrrrrrrrrrrryyyyyyy?" Coffee broke down the door to the other apartment. The inside of the room was demolished, a smoldering pit.

Coffee tore aside debris in the search for Larry. Everyone joined in.

"Hoooooowwwwww                    muuuuuuuccccccchhhhh loooooonnnnngggggeeeeerrrrrr wiiiilllllllllll weeeeee beeeee innnnnnn sllll-looooowwwww mooooottttttiiiiiiioooonnnn?" Snacks asked.

Lonnie looked at her watch. "Thhhhhhheeeeeeee saaaaaaaffffff-feeeeettttttttyyyyyyy sllllllooooooowwwwwwweeeeeeerrrrrr onnnnnnllllllllll-lyyyyyy          laaaaaaasssssssttttttttssssssss          onnnnnnneeeeeeee miiiiiinnnnnnnnuuuuuuuuutttttttteeeeeee."

Coffee lifted a smoldering briefcase and cradled Larry.

His blade was snapped in half, and the color had drained from his gem. The others looked on sullenly as Coffee tried to reconnect the pieces. After repeated failure, she turned to Lonnie and held them out.

Lonnie sadly prodded the pieces. "I'mmmm soooorrrrrrrrrrrrrryyyy Coooooofffffffffffeeeeeeeeee,          thhhhheeeeerrrrrreeeee'ssssss nooooooottttttttthhhhhhhiiiiiiiiinnnnnngggggg          tooooo          beeeeee dooooooonnnnnneeeee."

It was quiet.

Time returned to a normal speed, but no one spoke.

Coffee looked around the demolished room.

Lonnie put a hand on Coffee's shoulder. "I'm so sorry, Coffee." When she didn't get a response, she turned to the others. "She's programmed to protect us at all costs. Even if–"

"–Even if it means letting someone else die." Coffee cut her off.

They were all silent.

"There has to be something we can..." Kale stopped as Del put a hand on his shoulder and shook her head. A tear welled up in one of her eyes.

"I do not blame you." Coffee turned to Lonnie.

Lonnie nudged some of her charred possessions, and the remains of their new carpet, with her foot. "Do you want me to erase this from your memory?"

Coffee continued to stare at the pieces. "From what I've gathered, life for most people is at least 16% painful." Coffee looked up. "Even though it feels like only pain right now, it is not worth erasing. Not ever." Coffee touched a robotic finger to Lonnie's chin and gently lifted her head up so their eyes met. "But I'm afraid it is time for me to go."

"Are you sure?"

Coffee nodded and plunged a flash drive into her neck. "Based on your feedback, Coffee Two will have a reduced sarcasm drive and higher levels of obedience."

Lonnie tapped on her arm computer a few times. "Actually, I'd like this next version to remain as close to the original settings as possible." A tear fell down Lonnie's face. "And would you please add to the log that the last model was running the friendship sequence with 100% accuracy?"

Coffee handed Lonnie the flash drive, and the two of them embraced.

Coffee surveyed the rest of them and nodded. "Goodbye." She ran through one of the walls and leapt out into the night. It was a somber moment, but they took solace in the fact that the hole in the wall retained Coffee's shape, just like in a cartoon.

Snacks loudly blew his nose and used the same handkerchief to wipe away a steady stream of tears. Del patted him on the back. "How'd they even find us? Even with shared location that shouldn't be possible."

Lonnie cursed and kicked some of the rubble with her feet. "You know how I injected all of you with many, many things? Those *hypothetically* stop things from tracking you."

Kale crossed his arms. "I don't know which I like less, you operating on me or the way you said '*hypothetically*' just now."

Lonnie pawed through some debris and retrieved two singed halves of an egg. A partially-digested toe plopped out. "I'll save the technobabble, but I think this is how our location got tracked."

"Oh...how do we make sure they don't do it again?"

SPLAT!

Lonnie dropped a heavy piece of rubble on the toe and dusted her hands off. "That takes care of that. Now to take revenge on Evil Kale, assuming he's the one who did this, of course."

Del whistled from Kale and Snacks' apartment. "I know that everyone needs to grieve, but we've got a bigger problem..." She had pulled away the couch cushions and revealed a familiar sight: the portal, still intact. They raced back into the room.

"Coffee, bring up..." Lonnie stopped. She took the flash drive and stabbed it into her wrist computer.

An ancient startup chime was followed by Coffee's voice, but more singsongy and upbeat. "Hi there, Elonifred! I'm Coffee Two, your personal—"

"—Yeah, yeah, run a diagnostic on this portal."

"Happy to do so, I'll just need your password."

Lonnie typed on her arm.

"And for two-factor authentication, I'll need you to speak it aloud."

"Override."

"I'm afraid I can't do that."

"I will rip you apart!" Lonnie shook the device on her arm.

Del put her hands on her hips. "Lonnie, you've told me a dozen times that I need to have two-factor authentication on my devices."

"Time may be of the essence here!" Snacks urged as he examined the portal.

"Alright, alright." Lonnie whispered into her device.

"Hmm?" Coffee Two asked. "I can't hear that. You'll have to speak up."

She said it again, quietly. "And I know your microphones are sensitive enough to pick that up!"

"Buffering..." Coffee Two said quietly. "Please confirm you said the following: *'TESTICALSPECTICAL69.'*" This part was loud and in Lonnie's voice. Lonnie turned a new shade of anger. "Yes, or would you like to repeat that?"

"Yes." Lonnie grumbled before she turned back to the others, all of whom stifled pure childish laughter. "I needed to make it strange so I wouldn't forget it! Alright?" She glared at Coffee Two's pixelated face as it whistled innocently. "And now, go into settings and boost anxiety up to—"

"—Threat inbound," Coffee Two cut her off.

"Nice try, go..."

Suddenly, a holographic Earth projected from the screen. Their location was pinged with an orange dot, while a red dot rapidly approached. "Oh, don't mind me, please go back to your petty acts of revenge while a PlanetKiller is inbound." The sarcasm was so thick you could cut it with a knife. The red dot expanded and showed a missile hurtling toward them.

"Time to jump universes!" Snacks fished out some wires they had originally attached to the first portal.

"Wait!" Lonnie called out as he was about to connect them. "This portal is highly unstable. We might end up in a universe with no oxygen...or capitalism."

"Then let's explode it while it's still far away!" Del yelled as tension grew in the room.

"I'm afraid even at this distance, it will still obliterate us," Coffee Two replied.

They all turned to Kale.

He looked back at them in confusion. "What?"

"You've been quiet. Have any ideas?" Snacks asked politely.

"Uh...nothing. I have no ideas," he replied. "I'm literally the least qualified person, or robot, in this room."

"While you were dead and unconscious those times, we were talking, and we think we haven't given you enough of a chance to prove yourself," Del said warmly.

"Yeah, we don't want you to feel left out just because you're new to the Multiverse," Lonnie said encouragingly.

"That's nice, but really, I have nothing to contribute at this time! Please, someone else do something!" Kale looked around feverishly as the missile drew closer and closer.

"Go on, Kale. There are no stupid ideas." Snacks patted him on the back.

Since they didn't seem to budge, Kale said the first thing that came to his mind: "We could...just...ask it nicely to stop?"

Everyone was still for a moment before they burst into laughter.

"Alright, I lied when I said there were no stupid ideas!" Snacks howled.

Kale sourly crossed his arms. "New plan. We just let it destroy us."

"Now Kale, that sort of commentary is why we signed you up to see a therapist," Snacks replied.

Kale grumbled and pet his cat, Dog, who had slept through this entire ordeal.

As Lonnie wiped away a laughter-induced tear, she typed away on her arm. "Alright Coffee Two, activate protocol: '*If Kale Does Something Stupid 37*.'"

Suddenly, another layer of reinforced metal shutters closed on all open doors and windows. Kale nearly fell over as the floor opened up and fancy chairs emerged. The walls opened and revealed several panels full of colorful buttons, screens, and toggles.

Kale slowly turned his head to Lonnie "...'*If Kale Does Something Stupid...37*'?" He cradled his cat.

"It was before I really got to know you!" Lonnie replied defensively. "I just prepared for a few common scenarios that you, as someone new to the Multiverse, might stumble into. I was going to rename them, honest!"

Kale pouted. "I guess I really am new to Multiverse, because I didn't realize '*a few*' means '*37*'!"

Snacks grappled him into a swivel chair and clicked on his seatbelt. Lonnie used the opportunity to exit the conversation and take up the captain's chair.

"Boosters are primed!" Del yelled from a panel behind Lonnie.

Coffee Two spoke up. "There are actually 204 scenarios with similar naming schemes. Would you like me to rename them all?"

"*TWO HUNDRED AND FOUR–*"

At that moment, Lonnie flipped three switches above her head and pulled a red lever. The entire apartment lurched back, then rocketed forward with incredible force as Kale clung to a sleeping Dog.

After ten long seconds of this, they stopped. The shutters opened and Kale saw darkness...then a speck of blue and green in the distance. Kale stood up, much to Dog's annoyance. He gazed in wonder at the Earth, mesmerized by how peaceful and calm it was from this far away. "So, what's the plan? The missile follows us, and we deflect it from the Earth?"

Lonnie looked awkwardly at Kale. "Well..."

The Earth exploded.

A wave of force hit their apartment and knocked them all off balance.

Kale stumbled back, first from the force of the explosion, then from the realization that his planet had become fun-sized.

"Dang," Lonnie said. "I really liked that Earth."

"Good fries," Snacks said as the others nodded in agreement.

As Kale snapped back to reality, he realized their kitchen and living room now resembled a spaceship. "Evil Me did this..." Kale said aloud. "...So we, like, take him out?"

"Easy tiger." Lonnie helmed the ship with Del as her copilot. "I want that just as much as you, but see that blinking light? That means we're carrying an unstable portal, so our first priority is to find a way to close it." Lonnie pointed to a purple light on the dashboard. "Del, divert power to our side boosters, and balance that rear chemical tank out with a negative ion protocol."

"On it," Del replied without hesitation as she grabbed the wheel and twiddled a few dials.

"Snacks, can you navigate us using only planetary reflection coordinates while not engaging our omega-3 drive?"

Snacks was behind them at a station with hundreds of switches. He effortlessly reached across and flipped them with the speed of a 90-year-old court stenographer, "Like stealing babies from candy."

"And Kale..." Lonnie turned back to him. His station had one screen next to the cutlery drawer. "...You see that green dot on the screen?"

He nodded, ready to take orders.

"Let me know if you see any red dots." She turned back.

Kale's shoulders dropped, but then he shot up, a bit peeved. "Hey! I'm not completely useless you know! I can handle some actual responsibility!"

"It's an important job, bud," Snacks said as the others nodded along.

"Actually, I have a very important...uh...decoding job for you." Lonnie pressed a few buttons and a printer nearby sputtered out a grid of letters. Kale squinted at her, untrusting.

"Oh, that's a *very* important job!" Del exclaimed as if she was addressing a preschooler.

Kale hesitantly grabbed it. It was a wordsearch.

And worse, a wordsearch with words no longer than five letters. Kale glared at them and then got to work on it, not because he didn't see through their plan, but because he genuinely enjoyed wordsearches.

It was another five minutes before he finished. In that time, they had navigated through the debris of Earth and rerouted to another solar system.

By now, everyone was less tense and Lonnie finally let her headset rest around her neck. "Del, keep us on course with Coffee...Two." Lonnie stood and walked to the portal.

Catching a glint of discomfort, Kale joined her.

"I don't understand," Lonnie puzzled at the portal. "It was closed. The likelihood of another stray portal opening up in the same spot is infinitely small."

"So, someone or something has opened these portals on purpose?"

She shrugged. "That's not the least likely option. Luckily, I know someone who might be able to help us figure this out."

"And how're you feeling about Coffee?" Kale asked.

Lonnie took a moment. "We'd been through a lot together."

As she looked down, Kale put a hand on her shoulder. She reached up and squeezed it while the two looked into the black portal.

"Boop!" Coffee Two said. "By the way, that '*Boop*' means something is approaching!"

Both of them raced back to their seats.

"Kale, report!" Lonnie yelled.

He examined the screen. "Another dot is approaching the middle dot!"

"What color?"

"Green!"

Lonnie adjusted her mirror so they made eye contact. She sounded concerned. "Are you sure?"

He looked at it again. "Positive!"

Snacks squinted over at Kale's station. "That's definitely a *red* dot approaching us."

"It's the same color as the dot in the center!" Kale exclaimed whole-heartedly.

There was a moment where everyone was quiet.

"Kale...are you color blind?"

"I...I don't..."

Del snorted. "That would explain some fashion choices."

"Hey!" But before Kale could react, a loud explosion and the sound of catastrophic engine failure shifted his attention to the side.

He turned back just in time for Lonnie to stab him in the shoulder with a needle. He let out a whimpered cry. "Would you *please* stop stabbing me?" Kale's voice trailed off as his vision blurred and refocused.

His mouth hung agape as colors he had once thought the same now appeared completely different. He stammered out a "thank you" as he saw the two dots were, indeed, different colors.

It went unnoticed as Coffee Two projected a hologram in front of the refrigerator.

"Avast!" a bushy-bearded pirate hologram yelled. "Ye be flying through our territory! What be yer business?"

Noticing Lonnie's hand hovering over the "*Obliterate*" button, Snacks diplomatically interjected himself. "We're deeply sorry for intruding. If you send us the coordinates, we'll fly out immediately."

"Oh..." The pirate was taken aback. "Well, that'll be difficult because *all* space is our territory!" he yelled as other pirates cheered behind him.

Snacks squinted. "I mean...technically no, unless you mean in the sense that space belongs to everyone?" As Snacks said this, the other pirates murmured amongst themselves.

"Um...yes! That one!" The pirates cheered again.

"Then, by your own words, you're also in *my* territory." The pirates scratched their beards. "Unless—"

Lonnie sighed and pushed the button. Kale rose and watched from the window as a red (not green) missile revved up. Kale craned his neck to see the approaching pirates and found they didn't have a spaceship as he had imagined, but rather a large wooden boat with jets in addition to sails.

The flame of the missile grew wider and brighter until it finally shot off...and drifted pathetically toward the ship like the personified action of a sad trombone noise.

"What's that?" the assumed captain said as the missile drifted into a deckhand and bonked him in the eye. Other than an additional eyepatch needed, it had done little damage.

"Rats, I must've depleted our stock during takeoff." Lonnie sighed as she pulled a lever and they zoomed ahead.

Explosions rang out from the pirate ship as it gained on them. Cannonballs drifted past their apartment. "Prepare to be boarded and destroyed! We'll—"

Lonnie muted the hologram as the pirate continued. She stretched, "Anyone hungry?" The others nodded as Kale looked around bewildered.

"Shouldn't we be doing something to stop the pirates?!"

"Eh," Del replied. "We already encountered pirates earlier in our adventures. This seems like the same thing, but in space."

Snacks nodded. "Yeah, we fought them off pretty easily last time."

"What?! Last time we encountered pirates, they were splattered by the Kraken and you made me a giant! And last time I checked, there was no Space Kraken—is there a Space Kraken?"

Snacks nodded. "Yeah, but it's migrated space south for the space winter."

"Great. Now what should we do?" Kale asked frantically as he looked out the window at the wooden ship drawing closer.

They paused for a moment, and then Lonnie raised a finger like she had a great idea. "Ramen! We should do ramen, but like, the classy kind where we make the broth." They nodded.

A cannonball blasted through the wall, whizzing past Kale's face. He gestured to the hole as they crossed their arms.

"Kale..." Del cocked her head. "Is this *really* about making sure pirates don't kill us, or are you nervous about your therapy session in a few minutes and you want an excuse to get out of it?"

"How can I do therapy when we're being attacked by pirates?!" Kale exclaimed.

Snacks calmly diced mushrooms.

No one responded, so Kale felt obligated to keep talking. "Okay, maybe part of me doesn't want to do therapy, but that doesn't change the fact that pirates are literally trying to kill us!"

Snacks slid the mushrooms into the start of his broth. "Bud, if you promise to be on that call, I'll show you where the turret is."

"FINE!" Kale yelled as Snacks gestured to the carpet below his feet. Snacks then dropped a few chives. As he bent down to pick them up, a cannonball blasted through the spot where his head would've been.

Kale flung the carpet up and revealed a hatch. Lonnie tossed him a headset before he descended. "We love and appreciate you!" she called.

Kale grumbled the same thing back at them.

"Also, are you okay with soft-boiled eggs? If you don't respond I'm assuming you're okay with soft-boiled eggs!" Snacks yelled as Kale slammed the hatch shut.

He slid down the ladder into a small, spherical room with a turret. He leapt into the chair and seized the controls as he had seen in many science fantasy movies.

As he was about to figure out the controls, his phone rang. The caller ID read, *"Therapist."* Kale reluctantly put it on the headset.

"Hey, this is Kale. I know we have a session scheduled for right now, but I'm busy fighting pirates. And just to clarify, these aren't metaphorical pirates. They're real, and trying to kill us, and I just can't figure out the controls of this turret!"

There was a moment where Kale just flipped switches in silence, then a hearty voice responded. "Hey Kale, I absolutely understand. It sounds like you're going through a tough time right now." This caught Kale off guard. "I happen to know a lot about space warfare. You're first gonna need to take off the safety by pulling the lever to your left." The voice was older and calm, the sort of person Kale imagined had a well-trimmed white beard and frequently sat on logs overlooking bodies of water.

Sure enough, he could now move the turret around with ease. "Thanks..." he replied hesitantly. For some reason, he felt like this person was trying to trip him up, to trick him into saying something. Then he wondered why he had immediately gone to that place.

"Absolutely, this is your time and we can end whenever you want. I'm happy to just talk about turrets if that's alright with you. When you're ready to take a shot, push both buttons on either end of the wheel." Kale did, and a flurry of red energy cascaded near the pirate ship.

"It worked!"

"Awesome job. You're picking this up fast. Now, let's play around with some of those settings. Right now, it's probably on the default red blast with a '*bwoing*' sound, so let's try and get it to a turquoise and a '*pew-pew.*'

The next half hour flew by as Kale's therapist walked him through using the turret.

Together, they blasted away a barrage of incoming cannonballs and punched so many holes in the hull of the ship that the pirates eventually turned and fled. And even when the task was done, they continued to talk.

Kale shared about the anxieties of being thrust into the Multiverse with no prior knowledge, his confusing romantic feelings, dying and being brought back, Larry's death, and Coffee's departure.

His therapist laughed along with him, and they touched on how a hero complex, while noble, could actually create a barrier in his relationship with his friends if he valued them more than he valued himself. By the end, Kale wondered why he compared himself to others so frequently.

"By all means, compare apples to oranges, they're both fruits, and I bet you can find a lot of similarities..." his therapist started. "...But when an apple compares itself to how much it resembles an orange, rather than how good of an apple it can become, it loses the flavor that makes it special." This hit Kale like a baseball bat.

There was a beeping noise on the other end. "I'm afraid that's all the time we have for today. I'd like to talk again, but that's your decision."

Kale set up another appointment, and when he ended the call he let out a long sigh of relief. It felt, indeed, like his brain had just gotten a massage, in a way that no longer made him sick.

He emerged to the smell of delicious ramen, and everything seemed brighter. Maybe it was because it had taken this long for the color blindness serum to take full effect, but there can be more than one cat in a bag.

One of the big things he had talked about with his therapist was how he'd been suppressing romantic feelings for Lonnie for fear of ruining their friendship. Working through it, he had come to realize that eventually, it could boil over in unhealthy ways if he wasn't honest.

While Del and Snacks were on one corner of the roof space fishing, he readied himself to ask Lonnie out as she jotted down equations on the other side.

He had gone over it with his therapist, and the worst-case scenario was that she didn't share these feelings, but that would only be the end of their friendship if Kale was super weird about it.

At least, he believed that would be the worst-case scenario.

"Lonnie I–"

"–Your hands are sweaty." She squinted at him. "Are you having an allergic reaction to the serum?"

"No, it's–"

"–His heart is racing abnormally fast," Coffee Two chimed in.

Lonnie placed a hand on his forehead. "Coffee Two, take a blood sample."

A big mechanical arm with a syringe swung up from the roof and moved toward Kale. He ducked out of the way. "I'm just trying to ask you–"

Kale froze. A few seconds passed and neither of them could move. Panic set in as their eyes darted around.

"What's...happening...?" Kale struggled to get the words out.

At that moment, a moon–oh wait, it's actually a space station– appeared in front of them. It was massive and mechanical with a big red (not green) eye spotlighting down on them.

Coffee Two, also unable to move, changed the graphics of its face to a Magic 8-Ball. "*All signs point to imminent death.*"

# SIXTEEN

# An Avocado Is Technically A Berry

A woman's voice boomed from behind the large eye. "Release them, Tea 1,000."

They felt control of their bodies return and they stretched their tense muscles. Snacks held his fishing rod defensively, but Lonnie stopped him.

"It's alright, this is who we're here to see." Lonnie pressed a few buttons on her wrist and spoke into it. "Preparing to dock."

Now a robotic voice came through her computer: "Received. Who are your new friends? Vetting process initiated."

"Oh, come on–" Lonnie was cut off as all of them were jettisoned through space and toward the giant eye at top speed.

Kale closed his eyes as he was about to splatter into the ship.

When he opened them, he was seated in a nice, relatively modern living room with a splash of art deco.

A humanoid robot, with molded features that made it look way more advanced than Coffee or Coffee Two, surveyed him.

It placed a cup of tea next to him and tiredly pulled out a clipboard. "Sicknesses?"

"Hmm?" Kale looked around bewildered.

The robot seemed impatient. "Have you been sick recently?"

"I died a few days ago, and before that I was injected with a whole bunch of—"

"—I'll just mark '*no.*' Any fruits or vegetables to declare?"

Kale sipped the tea. It was bitter and oily. He pondered for a moment, then said, "Carrots?"

The robot looked over him, and then its head dropped with a low, heavy sigh. "Do you have any fruits or vegetables *on your person?*"

"Oh...no," Kale replied, embarrassed.

"Lovely. Enjoy the rest of my tea." The robot stood up and left the room before Kale could apologize.

At that same moment, another door opened and a middle-aged woman in a blue robe entered. She held the same clipboard as the robot and read from it. "Ah, Kale. How are you today?"

"Good. Sorry, I accidentally drank the tea of the—"

"—Apologizing is for the weak, dear. Now, I'm detecting a recent fluctuation in your anxiety. What's all that about?" She was very blunt and spoke so quickly Kale felt he must answer in turn.

"I recently was about to ask someone out, and—"

"—Follow." She waved her fingers and Kale obeyed. "I don't know you, but while you're here I can't have any sort of self-doubt. If there's someone you want to date, you date them. End of story." He followed closely behind her as they approached the door.

"I thought a relationship was about communication and a commitment to growth—"

She cut him off with a glare that somehow seemed familiar. "*I take what I want, and I can date whomever I like.* Repeat that back to me."

Kale uncomfortably obliged. Still, there was something uplifting about her intensity and raw faith in him.

The door opened, and she nodded forward. "Good. Know you can be with whoever you want...except *that one*, of course," she whispered and pointed ahead to Lonnie. "She's the most brilliant creature in the Multiverse, so, of course, you'll never be on her level. But you can date anyone else, I'm sure."

Kale felt a pit in his stomach, but he remembered what his therapist had told him about valuing himself. Plus, it wasn't like this lady had any sort of credibility or intimate knowledge of Lonnie. A milestone in his mental health, he managed to push the self-doubt away.

Lonnie turned to the two of them. "Hey Mom."

Kale felt like he had just dropped his ice cream cone in the middle of the zombie apocalypse: more important things were going on, but he was still sad and couldn't say anything for fear of being eaten alive.

Lonnie's mother opened her arms for a hug, but she did not step forward. Kale, an expert on awkward interactions, could immediately feel Lonnie's discomfort as she hoverhanded her way around the hug.

"So, I've run a full schematic over this portal and can't figure out–"

"–Dear, why do you wear those overalls? They're greasy and don't flatter your figure." Her mother tugged at the jean fabric. "I've sent you dresses. Why don't you wear them?"

"No pockets, Mom." Lonnie didn't look up from her own clipboard, "Have you noticed any obtuse frequencies recently? Anything that might explain the reappearance of a portal or leak?"

Lonnie's mom didn't seem to notice her daughter, and instead narrowed her eyes on the opposing doors through which Snacks and Del entered. "And these must be your friends!"

Snacks stepped forward, charisma blasters fully charged. "The name's Knightly, Snacks Knightl–"

Lonnie's mom put her hand over Snacks' face and turned to Del. "Deloise, lovely to see you. Has my daughter been getting you into trouble?"

Del just laughed uncomfortably.

"Mom, this is serious. Earth was just blown up and the universe itself could be on the verge of collapse!" Lonnie said, a trickle of anger leaking through the dam.

"Oh, I know what your father would say about that..." Lonnie's mom said in a demeaning tone.

As Lonnie crossed her arms, Kale moved next to her, as did the others...though Snacks cowered a bit behind Del.

"Listen, either you can help us figure this out, or we'll leave and find someone else who can." Lonnie planted her feet firmly on the ground.

"Is that so?" Her mom smiled. "Tea 1,000, initiate *Empty Nester*

*Protocol!*" Suddenly, all the windows and doors slammed shut. A malicious grin stretched across the face of Lonnie's mother. "Now, we're all going to look at Lonnie's baby photos, then we'll sit down to a long dinner where I'll drink half a bottle of wine and critique everyone's life choices!"

She laughed maniacally as a dozen different Tea 1,000 robots appeared in the room. "But first, Lonnie, why don't you put on this nice dress I bought you?"

"I told you, Mom..." Lonnie shifted her hands around as the Tea 1,000s encroached upon them. "...Most dresses don't have POCKETS!" Lonnie reached into her overalls and retrieved a banana, holding it forward threateningly as if it were a gun.

Lonnie's mom squinted at her, confused. "Sweetie, I think you've gone a bit bonkers..."

"Have I?" Lonnie smiled.

"Undeclared fruits and/or vegetables detected," the Tea 1,000s all said uniformly. "I have failed. Self-termination commencing. Oh, bother." They let out a collective sigh, and all their heads exploded.

Another mechanical voice called out over the loudspeaker, "Now crafting Tea 1,001."

By the time the rest realized what happened, Lonnie had ripped a circuit board out of a computer and opened the door to their docked apartment.

As the gang retreated, Lonnie's mom called after them, "Very clever. Guess where you get that from?"

"Seeya at Christmas, Mom!" Lonnie yelled.

The spaceship took off with the sound of scraping metal.

"She seems nice," Snacks said. "Would've been great if she helped us figure out the portal, though."

Lonnie held up the circuit board slyly. "Oh, she will." She bit into her banana.

Kale looked on with admiration. He didn't even notice that when Lonnie flung the banana peel behind her, it just missed the garbage can and landed subtly next to it. This detail will absolutely not be important later in this adventure, and you should purge it from your mind at this very moment.

"Any idea how long it'll take to...process...or whatever?" Kale asked.

Lonnie shook her head. "We'll need a hefty power source to over-clock the micron—to do the thing. Luckily, I have another contact who lives nearby." Lonnie dialed a phone number and held her wrist to her ear.

Kale imagined all the ferocious three-headed, claw-wielding monsters that might be Lonnie's contact, and yet, none of them seemed as intimidating as her mom.

"Yeah, we'll be there soon. Bye, Dad."

And they say Kale's anxiety grew three sizes that day.

Kale tried to ask Lonnie questions and find a good time to talk about feelings 'n' stuff, but she and Del were busy with the portal.

Snacks knowingly patted him on the back, and they went space fishing off the roof. "Meeting parents is stressful. You good?"

"Yeah."

They sat in comfortable silence for a bit longer.

"So, bananas are fruit?" Snacks puzzled.

"Yeah. Isn't it technically a nut or a berry or something because it doesn't have seeds?"

"Oh, it does have seeds. We watched that thing on how they've become super tiny through selective breeding."

"Right, it was after we wondered if GMOs were actually bad for us. Were they?"

"Nah, but there's a lot more sugar in everything, and there's a higher risk of—"

"Monocropping!" they both said in unison.

"Good times," Kale replied as the two stared out into the abyss. He raised a fist to Snacks, who instinctively bumped it. "Thanks, man."

"Always, my dude."

They didn't catch anything as they flew through some floating cul-de-sacs and landed in front of a lightly bouncing one-story house. It was a little run-down and had a front garden decorated with the most eclectic collection of lawn gnomes Kale had ever seen.

The moment they stepped out, Lonnie was wrapped up in a bear hug by a burly man with shaggy hair and a soul patch. He seemed more excited than a dog that had just been reunited with its owner. Kale felt more relaxed. He had time to prepare, so there wouldn't be any surprises.

And then, of course, her dad spoke. Kale's eyes went wide. This man's voice was familiar, very familiar.

It was his therapist.

"Kale..." Lonnie's dad paused. "...Nice to meet you!"

Kale breathed a sigh of relief. A decent percentage of their session had been devoted to asking Lonnie out. He decided to keep his talking to a minimum so his voice wouldn't be recognized.

Lonnie hooked up a powerline to the apartment spaceship as her dad bustled them inside. There were pictures of Lonnie everywhere, a stark contrast from the previous home. "Whoops!" he yelled as he fanned a smoking waffle maker. "I hope ya like 'em well done!"

"Dad, we're here on business. We don't have time to...eat...waffles..." By the time Lonnie finished her sentence, the others had flocked to the table and seated themselves hungrily. She shrugged and had a seat.

"Hmmm...interesting..." Lonnie's dad nodded as they recapped what they knew about the portal. "It's very unlikely to be a random occurrence. It could be...no..."

Lonnie sighed. "What is it, Dad?"

"Well, we attribute stray portals as a sign that The Multiverse Is Leaking...but why? Catalyst Theory states that they pop up during events that completely change the expected direction of the Multiverse."

He went to the bookshelf, waffle in hand. "Ah, here it is. *Stray portals have been discovered after two people, who normally would never meet, collide. Notable cases include: the convergence of Lord Spaghettus The Wise and Meatballe McBalle, Those Two Dudes Who Both Wore Stripes On The First Day Of Class, and Martha Stewart and Snoop Dogg.'"*

"So..." Del looked over the book. "Hypothetically speaking, if two people, like soulmates, were destined to fall in love and be together forever, that could be what's feeding the portal?" She looked between Kale and Lonnie, who promptly did everything they could not to make eye contact.

"Yes, that could absolutely be what's causing the portal. But for it to reach this level of instability, the two would have to remain in contact for some time, at least the amount of time it would take for a series of adventures with a colorful cast of characters." As he went to do dishes, everyone excused themselves and quickly filed out of the room.

Kale was about to sneak away when Lonnie's dad made an "Ahem."

"Great waffles..." was all Kale could think to say as he nervously turned around.

"So? How'd it go?" he said, monotone.

"Uhh...what are you referring to?"

Lonnie's dad got real close and raised an intimidating eyebrow at Kale. "You think I wouldn't recognize my own client's voice?"

"Right...is this the part where you chase me out of here with a shotgun and tell me to stay away from your daughter?"

"Kale, that is...such an outdated way of looking at things." He clapped Kale on the shoulder and smiled. "You, young man, are quite the catch, and my daughter is an adult who can date whoever she likes. Plus, who needs a shotgun when you have the most powerful weapon in the world: words."

A wave of relief washed over Kale.

"But I do want to know something. Are you prepared...sexually?"

Kale screamed internally. At this point, he would've preferred the shotgun.

"I...I..." Kale looked around and saw a shadow loom over the front lawn.

POW! A laser blast exploded. Bits of grass and lawn gnome flew in every direction.

Kale had never been happier about his potential imminent destruction.

## SEVENTEEN

## A Friend Like Me

---

They all raced to the window from the other rooms. Del sighed and walked out the front door, with the others cautiously following in tow.

"I said a warning shot! Don't actually hit them!" A loud microphone echoed from a massive spaceship above them. The voice was familiar. "This is the Department of Multiverse Ventures. Come out with your hands–oh, you're already outside. Hi everyone!"

"Hey Wixby," they all replied in a state of post-waffle fullness.

The door to the spaceship opened and, from a very long escalator, Wixby emerged. "Sorry about your lawn!"

"Accidents happen," Lonnie's dad said without a care as he raked up ceramic lawn gnome shards.

"So..." Wixby looked over them. "We received a report of a stray portal that's about to implode, ending the Multiverse as we know it."

"You mean '*the universe*,' right?" Lonnie replied.

"Like an unwicked rope on a sailing barge, I'm *a frayed knot*." Wixby chuckled to himself, as did Del. "But seriously, if we don't close this portal soon, it will literally kill everyone, everywhere, forever...and that's illegal."

"Great. How do we close it?" Lonnie asked Wixby.

Wixby looked behind him and saw no one. "Oh, you're asking me? No idea."

"Can we ask your boss? Someone at the head of the company?" Snacks asked.

Wixby smiled. "Actually, I am the boss. Everyone else died!"

"Congratulations!" Del replied enthusiastically.

"Thanks! So, does anyone know how to close it?"

There was a moment of silence before Lonnie's dad spoke up. "Well, the theory is that this portal is caused by an unlikely convergence between two parties. We need to stabilize the future in order for it to close, so I see two options: we find those two and separate them forever...OR we sit them both down and have a long and awkward conversation about the future."

Kale and Lonnie made eye contact.

"...Or we just do science at it until it's fixed!" Lonnie yelled as she rushed toward their apartment with the others in tow.

Lonnie's dad grabbed Kale by the shoulder. "Remember, words are your greatest weapon," he said ominously before turning to Wixby. "Well, this ragtag group seems to have everything under control. Waffles?"

"Waffles!" Wixby replied as the two of them headed into the house.

By the time Kale caught up, microchips and bolts were flying through the air as the three others shouted scientific jargon. The group was more panicked than Kale had ever seen.

Kale sighed. "Lonnie, this is silly. We should just–"

Lonnie raised a finger to him without looking up. "I know what you're going to say, and whatever you do, *don't*."

"The entire Multiverse could end unless we talk this out. I'm just trying to see if you wanna go on a da–" Kale was cut off as Lonnie pressed some buttons and an airbag ejected from his flannel, one of many features Lonnie had installed on his body.

He struggled for a minute before it deflated. "Lonnie, will you go out with me?"

Before either of them could say a word, a cloud of purple smoke burst forward from the far side of the room. The sound of thunder and deep laughter echoed from inside until a humanoid figure appeared.

"Oh no," Lonnie whispered. "It's the Define-The-Relationship Genie!"

The Genie laughed. It resembled the type found in Disney's *Aladdin*, but was distinctly different enough that they wouldn't sue for likeness. "So...do you two really want to risk your friendship over this?"

"Well I–" Kale was cut short as Lonnie tackled him. A beam of energy shot from the Genie's mouth and narrowly missed them both.

"We have to dodge those questions!" Lonnie yelled as they scampered to their feet.

The Genie laughed, "If you two broke up, would the friend group have to pick sides? Wouldn't that ruin....*game night*?"

Kale sidestepped as Lonnie grabbed a broom. She began to sweep at the Genie. "Hurry! Help me sweep these questions under the rug!" It appeared to do very little to the Genie, so she tried to hit it with the broom.

Kale puzzled at her. "Lonnie, if you don't wanna go out, that's completely fine."

"I...think I do. I just figured we would start off casual and undefined, and then later down the line figure all this out! I mean, what if we have some kind of nasty breakup? Or you get comfortable and let slip you're a racist?!" At that moment, a beam of energy shot out of her mouth and Kale barely ducked out of the way. "Back me up here, folks!" Lonnie yelled to Del and Snacks.

"We're definitely staying out of this," Del replied calmly. The two of them had moved to the other side of the room and shared a bag of pistachios.

The Genie laughed. "Yes...good...let the fear take over you. Imagine if Kale's cat gets really attached to you, Lonnie. Then one day you're gone, and the cat dies of a broken heart!"

Lonnie nodded in agreement. It was the first nonsensical thing Kale had seen her do.

Kale stood up as heavy winds swirled around him. "That wouldn't happen! Partially because I'm pretty sure my cat is pure evil–"

"–Most cats are!" Snacks interjected without looking up.

"...But you're one of my closest friends. How could we not hang out all the time?" As Kale said this, a bit of light energy sparkled from his hands, but the dark purple cloud enveloped Lonnie and most of the apartment.

The Genie grew larger and now barely fit in the room. "What if you two realize you're not actually attracted to each other? What if that just happens to one of you, and they have to break up with the other, and the rest of the friend group resents them? What if you buy a birthday present for the other, and then you break up with them? Do you still give them the present?!" The Genie laughed maniacally as the two dodged the blasts.

On the last attack, Lonnie froze. Without hesitation, Kale leapt between her and the Genie and raised his hands to brace the impact. "It could all happen!" he yelled.

He felt the cold energy of the Genie strike, but when he looked up, there was a shield of golden energy that blocked the ongoing blast of energy.

"Everything that's been said and worse could happen. Heck, we might even move in with each other, and then it hits the fan, and we're both forced to awkwardly live under the same roof until our lease is up!" Kale yelled this as the wind blew his hair backward. The light energy grew flickered and struggled against the Genie. "Everything is uncertain, and maybe this is a mistake, but I still want to try!"

The Genie grunted and doubled its efforts. "Imagine if you had kids. Then you'd be forced to be together at least until they turned 18!"

Kale felt himself slide backward, but then a hand on his shoulder stopped him.

"Actually, it would be better for our imaginary kids if we just got a divorce at that point. But we still remained amicable and had open lines of communication!" she yelled as the light energy grew stronger.

The entire room shook as energy extended from their hands.

Kale yelled into the energy, "And...at...that...point...we...could... probably...still...do...combined...holidays!"

The two clasped their free hands together, and a blast of light energy extended from their palms. The Genie let out a shriek as it collapsed into nothingness. The two panted.

"So..." Lonnie started. "Wanna grab coffee sometime?"

"Yeah." Kale gasped for breath. "Something casual."

The two hugged.

Behind them a silvery rainbow shone, and a plump woman in a pink dress with wings fluttered through. "Hello!" she said in a squeaky voice. "I am the Should-We-Have-Kids Fairy, and wouldn't now be a great time to figure out—"

Kale and Lonnie looked at each other and, together, they kicked the fairy out the open door, into the dark recesses of space. She exploded into a million pieces of glitter as they high-fived.

"Aww," Snacks said warmly as he looked upon the two of them.

"I ship it," Del said.

"*Space*ship it," Snacks added as the four of them laughed like it was the end of an old sitcom.

"Not to be *that* robot, but the portal is still here...and it appears to be growing more erratic by the minute." Coffee Two's mechanical arm pointed to the portal, which now pulsated.

"I don't understand," Del said.

"I do." Lonnie turned to Kale. "Kale, we need to make out."

"Okay."

"You don't need to know the scientific reasoning behind why making out can center our universe and repair the leak?"

"Nah."

"Alright then."

Lonnie and Kale leaned in and time seemed to slow, but just metaphorically. As their lips were about to collide, an engine noise revved outside the house. Suddenly, a figure on a motorcycle crashed through the wall.

As everyone picked themselves up, a familiar voice chuckled.

"Looks like I got here just in time." It was Kale, on a motorcycle, with a puka shell necklace.

"Evil Kale..." Snacks muttered under his breath.

# EIGHTEEN

# The Big War Sequence

"Coffee Two, defensive measures!" Lonnie yelled. One of Coffee Two's mechanical arms descended from the ceiling with a large pipe.

"Override," Evil Kale said calmly.

"I swear...this never...happens..." Coffee Two replied as the arm, and pipe, went limp.

At the same time, Snacks flung a wrench at Evil Kale, who deflected it with ease and stepped closer.

"Fools," Evil Kale chuckled. "Now I–"

–BANG! BANG! BANG!

The others looked over at Del as she held up a smoking handgun. Evil Kale fell to the ground.

The other three slowly craned their heads to her. "Del, what the f**k? When did you get a gun?!"

She shrugged. "What? I borrowed it from work. You would not believe how good these little murder clickers are for business." Del waved the gun around until Lonnie snatched it from her hands. Del peered over Evil Kale's body. "Take that, ya ugly bastard."

"Hey!" Kale replied.

"Right...sorry."

"Is that the best you got?" A low growl echoed from Evil Kale as he stood back up, completely healed.

Kale pushed himself in front of the others. "Listen, Evil Me. It's me you want. There's no need to involve the others." Behind him, the others groaned. "...And not because I have a hero complex, but because objectively this seems like the best scenario."

The others reconsidered their groans.

Evil Kale laughed. "I see why they call you '*Good Kale*'..."

"We do?" Snacks replied.

Evil Kale puzzled at them. "Well...I'm Evil Kale, and he's literally my opposite. I'm evil, he's good. I'm a night owl, and he's a morning person. I'm smart, he's..." It was an unfortunate time for Kale to be picking wall debris out of his nose. "...Different."

"Huh?" Kale looked up, confused.

"Do you not even know how you came to exist?" Evil Kale stepped in closer. "When I decided to conquer the Multiverse, I plucked all the weakness from my body, and you were created. A person made of nothing but insecurities, anxieties, and doubts. But you've impressed me by making it this far. Join me, and together we will rule the Multiverse and bring about an age of unfounded destruction!"

Kale considered this, perhaps a little too long. Actually, it got to the point where Snacks had to nudge him. "Probably nah. Do you have dental?"

"It's more of an unpaid internship!"

"You monster!" Kale yelled.

At that moment, Lonnie lunged forward and attempted to kiss Kale, but the two felt themselves held in place as Evil Kale extended a hand in their direction. He smiled. "Not so fast there."

"If we don't make out...the Multiverse will implode. And that includes you!" Lonnie yelled.

"I'm very aware." Evil Kale walked forward and yanked Lonnie's computer from her arm and pressed some buttons. Kale felt gravity surge past his face as Evil Kale telekinetically flung Del and Lonnie out of the hole in the wall.

He pressed more buttons on Lonnie's wrist computer and metal shutters blocked every remaining way in or out.

Kale looked away to shield himself from the force and realized that Snacks was still behind him. He struggled against the energy with his boots clamped to the floor.

Evil Kale smiled and flicked his wrist. Snacks' boots unclasped and he tumbled, in his socks, all the way to his room. The door slammed shut after him. Kale knew Snacks would not be able to open the door without his boots. He assumed this was part of some curse that made it so he could only kick down doors, but he'd never asked.

Kale felt his body release, and he could move freely as Evil Kale walked past him to examine the portal. It pulsated like a beating heart and the edges became increasingly blurred. "I wonder what it will be like, to destroy the Multiverse."

Kale didn't know what to say. There were no magic swords, no robots, and no friends with special abilities. He was completely alone. Kale eyed a chair which had broken in the tumble. He looked from the sharp, splintered end to Evil Kale.

"Aren't you going to try and attack me? Go on, take your best shot." Evil Kale sneered at him, but he didn't even bother to turn around.

Kale's foot brushed a stray ping-pong ball, knocked loose from some crevasse during their recent escapades. It reminded him of the skill he was best at, and he got an idea...which was never a good thing.

"How about this?" Kale stood on the opposite end of the room as the couch. "If I can make this shot directly into the portal, you don't destroy the Multiverse. Deal?"

Evil Kale looked at him. "No."

"Oh."

"Did...did you really think that would work?"

In lieu of an answer, Kale aimed and threw the ping-pong ball with all his might.

It went wide. Like five feet away from the portal.

Kale sighed and sat on the far end of the couch. "So, I'm really a clone? Made from all the parts you didn't want?"

Evil Kale chuckled. "Yes."

"Like the plot of *Twins* starring Arnold Schwarzenegger and Danny DeVito?"

"I don't...I haven't seen that movie...but thanks for the spoiler."

Kale crossed his arms. "Oh, were you planning on watching it in the next few minutes before you end the Multiverse?"

"Whatever," Evil Kale muttered. "Regardless, don't you think it's odd you have no long-term memories, no family?"

Kale shrugged. "I mean, when you say it like that...but I do have a family."

Evil Kale shook his head and continued to laugh. "Of all the Kales I've killed, you've taken it the best."

Something clicked with Kale. He remembered what Lonnie's dad/his therapist had said about words being his best weapon. "Hey man, since we're both about to die, why *did* you kill all the other Kales?"

"Because I wanted to!" His voice was shrewd, and he continued to laugh like a poorly-written supervillain.

"Yeah...but why?"

"TO DESTROY THEM!"

"But, dude...why?"

Evil Kale paused for a moment. "I don't...really know..."

"Well, do you like it? Maybe it's a hobby, like scrapbooking..."

"Or genocide!"

"...Or bowling?"

"...I wouldn't know. I've never been bowling."

"Really? I'm literally a clone made from your garbage parts, and even *I've* been bowling."

"Well, it's a group activity..."

Kale and Evil Kale locked eyes for a moment before Kale spoke. "Do you wanna go bowling?"

Evil Kale looked completely confused. "I wouldn't want to impose. Plus, I have a Multiverse to crush."

"It'd be no imposition. In fact, I think we get a group discount the more people there are."

"Or we just KILL all those who run the bowling alley, and bowl for FREE!" Evil Kale laughed.

"...Or we could *not* kill them..."

Evil Kale cocked his head, confused. "You want to...*not* kill someone?"

"I mean, not if it'll be a huge imposition—"

"—No, no, it's fine. It's just...no one's ever asked me not to kill before."

Kale considered this. At that moment, he saw himself in this amalgamation of wickedness. "Evil Kale, would you please not end the Multiverse?"

There was a long moment where the two Kales stared at each other.

"'K..." Evil Kale replied.

"*Forreal?*"

"Five real." Evil Kale smiled. "Now, let's close this portal and go bowling, and then maybe we can watch *Twins* starring Arno–OW!" Evil Kale was hit in the head with a broom. Not enough to do any damage, but the bristles were quite annoying.

Snacks brandished the broom at them, barefoot, bruised, and bloody. "Run Kale! Specifically, regular non-evil Kale!"

Kale pushed himself between Snacks and Evil Kale. "It's alright. Evil Kale's good now."

Snacks squinted at Evil Kale who waved innocently. "Evil Kale...is good?"

Both Kales shrugged in unison. "Apparently, people *don't* like it when you murder them and collapse their universe. Who'da thunk it? I think I'll still go by 'Evil Kale,' though. I've already put it on so many forms."

Kale looked from Snacks to the open door and noticed it hadn't fallen or been kicked off its hinges. "Snacks, you opened a door to try and save me?"

Snacks squinted at the two of them. "Yes?"

"I mean...I thought you couldn't open doors, like you were cursed or something. Isn't that why you always kick down doors?"

"Cursed? Do you think curses are real?" Snacks chuckled. "I kick doors down because doorknobs have a ton of germs."

Evil Kale smirked. "Man, it's like looking in a really dumb mirror."

Kale flung his arms up. "Whatever."

Evil Kale opened the shutters, and the three of them peered out over a huge battlefield with thousands of fighters. There were pirates, dragons, documentarians, and DMV employees...pretty much everyone they had come across in their adventures.

Then Lonnie rode a majestic Goobasaurus in front of them, brandishing a sword as her voice carried over the field. "And though alone we are weak, like single strands of spaghetti, together we are strong, like many strands of spaghetti! The fate of the Multiverse and everything we hold dear is decided today! Will you fight?!"

Her booming voice was met with loud cheers from the many armies. Then she glimpsed back and saw the three of them awkwardly waving.

"It's cool." Kale gave a thumbs-up. "We talked it out."

"Yeah?" she replied.

"Yeah," Snacks assured her.

Lonnie stopped and looked from the three of them to the army. "So, change of plans. Everyone can go home. Sorry for any inconvenience."

Loud, disappointed "awws" echoed through the battlefield as everyone dispersed.

"I can kill some of them if we want? It's really no big deal," Evil Kale whispered.

Kale shook his head as Lonnie dismounted and approached them cautiously. Evil Kale handed her back the wrist computer.

"Kale thought curses were real!" Snacks chuckled.

They went inside. Evil Kale poked and prodded the couch before looking up at Kale and Lonnie. "Now, would you two hurry up and close this portal? We have bowling to get to!"

The two looked at each other. Background music swelled, and they leaned in. Of course, they miscalculated and bumped schnozzes, but then their lips met, and they totally made out. Both smiled as they backed up.

There was a quiet peace. A catharsis for Kale, in particular, who had returned to the same place he started this adventure, but with a newfound wisdom he could carry through life.

"Well, that didn't work." Snacks pointed to the portal, just as strong as it had been moments before.

"That should've done it." Lonnie examined the portal.

"Better round the bases to make sure," Del said jokingly as she stepped into the room, brandishing a waffle. "What'd I miss?"

A flash of panic stretched across Evil Kale's face. "There's less time than I thought." He pointed to a pot near the sink. "If we don't fill this pot with water right now, the entire Multiverse will collapse!" Kale grabbed the pot as he was the closest to the sink.

"Oh no!" He tried to fit the pot under the faucet, but he couldn't. "There are dirty dishes in the sink and no room for me to fill up the pot!"

Evil Kale slumped down. "Then all hope is lost."

In a fraction of a second, the portal expanded rapidly enough to encapsulate the entire Multiverse, obliterating everything inside it.

Everyone dies.

The End.

## NINETEEN

# Deus Ex Machina

---

T he unfortunate reality is that not doing your dishes in a timely manner is the most common reason for complete Multiversal collapse. But because ending the story there did not test well with our market of vampires 218-234, this story picks up in a similar Multiverse. Most events unfolded in the exact same way, however, in this setting the dishes had been done. Also, everyone's really into electro-jazz.

A FLASH OF PANIC STRETCHED ACROSS EVIL KALE'S FACE. "THERE'S LESS time that I thought." He pointed to a pot near the sink. "If we don't fill this pot with water right now, the entire Multiverse will collapse!" Kale grabbed the pot as he was the closest to the sink.

"Easy peasy, lemon squeezy!" Kale moonwalked to the sink and easily filled the pot.

Evil Kale soaked the portal in the pot. It pulsated and shrunk a little bit. "That'll buy us a minute or two, but this thing is ready to blow." Evil Kale turned to Kale and Lonnie. "Are you two sure you're cool?"

They both kinda shrugged and nodded.

"We could make out more?" Kale put forward. Del subtly low-fived him.

Evil Kale stroked his stubble. "It doesn't make sense. In romantic comedies, once the two kiss everything is resolved."

"Unless..." Lonnie's eyes flashed as she typed on her keyboard. "Coffee Two, show me a timeline of portal energy."

"Would a '*please*' or a '*thank you*' really hurt you so much?" Coffee Two projected a graph in front of them. There were many bumps and peaks, but Lonnie zoomed in on the first large peak and read the date aloud.

"Ah, so that's the day you two met," Evil Kale said.

"No..." Lonnie took a step back as the portal swelled and made a high-pitched pre-implosion sound. "We'd met before, but that was the day–"

"–Oh! I've got it!" Snacks addressed the group excitedly. "That was the first day that Kale and I..." Snacks turned to Kale. "The day we first..."

The two locked eyes and their bewilderment simultaneously became understanding. "...Started watching *The Office*!"

Kale's eyes lit up. "Exactly! And every one of these peaks is probably a time where we were watching *The Office* as well!"

The other four, including Coffee Two, exchanged bemused looks. There were several false starts as the group buffered through the stupidity and tried to get a word in.

"Just give them a minute, they'll figure it out..." Del surveyed Kale and Snacks as they frantically moved around the room.

"Hurry everyone!" Kale yelled. "We have to watch *The Office*!"

"I'm making popcorn!" Snacks replied from the kitchen.

"...Or not." Del let out a long sigh.

With all of his might, Kale pushed buttons on the remote to queue up the next episode. Snacks dove next to him, bowls of popcorn in hand. The others just stared.

"What are you all waiting for?" Kale asked, his mouth full of popcorn. "The fate of the Multiverse depends on us watching TV right now!"

In their defense, as they watched TV together, the portal had ceased to swell and the explodey noise had lessened.

Evil Kale stood in front of the television. "Do you two not see what's happened?"

"We can't *see* because you're *IN FRONT OF THE TELEVISION!*" Snacks threw popcorn at Evil Kale as the two craned their heads around him.

Still, Evil Kale continued, his voice ominous and deep. "A prophecy foretold of two beings who are destined to be together. It's an eternal bond so great, an epic bromance so strong, that their intertwined paths may be the single most important event to ever happen across the entire Multiverse." He seemed to finally have their attention. "I believe you two are those beings, and with that, you carry immense power. Both of you may be responsible for the survival or destruction of everything in existence."

All was quiet.

"Neat," Snacks replied.

"Salt?" Kale asked as Snacks handed it to him.

"We're doomed," Lonnie concluded as the portal once again started to vibrate and grow.

"So, like, what d'we have to do to fix ol' portal-y?" Snacks licked his fingers and pointed a thumb at the portal next to him.

"Well..." Lonnie squinted and did some mental calculations.

Kale knew the answer, and the longer he put it off, the more awkward it would become. He set his popcorn on the coffee table and kissed Snacks right on the lips.

Snacks gasped and pulled away. "Dude?!"

"Now it's done and over with. Multiverse saved. You're welcome." Kale wiped his lips.

The others suppressed their laughter.

"What?" Kale replied hesitantly.

Lonnie chuckled. "I was gonna suggest you two just plan a trip together, y'know, to stabilize the timeline...but this works as well, I guess!" She pointed to the portal, which was now considerably smaller.

"Next time, please lead with that information." Kale buried his head in his hands.

"*Next time*?!" Snacks scooched back. "And why did that work? Do I have to date Kale now?!"

Coffee Two jabbed Kale in the side a few times. "I estimate that one act stabilized the timeline because it will provide years of material with which we can make fun of Dopey Kale."

Kale sunk deeper into the couch. "...Don't you mean *Good* Kale?"

Coffee Two shook its face. As everyone else laughed at him, the portal shrunk to about the size of a ping-pong ball.

"Okay, fine." Kale addressed everyone. "Now the portal is stable, and we don't need to make fun of me anymore."

"Actually..." Evil Kale put on some sparkly gloves. "This portal isn't the type that'll ever close. It'll need to be continually resupplied with timeline anchors, such as a series of comical and escalating adventures with a close group of friends."

Everyone groaned, "That seems like a lot of work."

Evil Kale smiled. "Well, it's not so hard...if you're all dead!" Before anyone could react, Evil Kale blasted them with telekinetic energy from his sparkly gloves. Everyone flew across the room and landed in a pile in the corner.

"Ow!" Kale rubbed his face. "I thought you weren't evil anymore, Evil Kale?!"

Evil Kale took out a container and smugly bottled the portal. "I guess you can say I have a villain complex because I...lied!"

Everyone gasped.

"You're a monster!" Snacks yelled.

"And ugly!" Del added.

"Hey!" Kale added.

"Sorry...again..."

"Thanks for stabilizing the portal. With this as a fuel source, I will rule the Multiverse! Now, why don't you all make like a tree...and die!" Evil Kale raised his hands toward them. They struggled, unable to move forward as a bright red light from his hands expanded.

With no escape in sight, everyone hugged. A quiet moment before the end.

Suddenly, a large, mechanical figure burst through the wall, punching Evil Kale in the face. He flew out of the living room and into the kitchen as the original Coffee stood there triumphantly. "Stay away from my meatsacks, you butthole!"

Everyone got to their feet, no longer affected by the telekinesis and stood behind Coffee.

"I am Coffee. You killed someone I love. I will now destroy you," Coffee said calmly as she charged up a blast in her hand cannon.

Evil Kale stood and wiped a bit of blood from his temple. He sneered at them. "Fools, you may have figured out my weakness of being punched in the face, but this won't be the last you see of me!" Evil Kale inched backward, the bottled portal in one hand and swirly red energy in the other.

"You won't get away with this!" Kale yelled.

Evil Kale chuckled as he continued backward to the exit. "Oh, but I will! I've now ascended to the status of Big Bad Evil Guy in your adventures! I'll cause enough chaos and destruction to, let's say, fill at least a trilogy of books, maybe up to seven! Your group of adventurers will always find themselves in predicaments, and you know who'll be behind it all? Me! And toward the end, will my actions not make as much sense? Possibly! But at that point, we'll all just go with it because we've sunk too much time into this to question it or stop now! Prepare yourselves for the beginning of a wild and–"

At that moment, Evil Kale stepped backward onto Lonnie's banana peel from earlier, which, if you'll remember, did not land in the rubbish bin, but directly beside it.

His head hit the edge of the counter with a breaking sound that made all of them, even Coffee, recoil. The banana peel flew up in the air and landed on Evil Kale's face.

They stood around, dumbfounded, as a pool of blood quickly spread around Evil Kale's lifeless body.

"Well then..." Lonnie started.

They continued to stand around. Snacks coughed.

"Anyone wanna watch *The Office*?" Everyone nodded.

Coffee dug into her cloak and handed a shiny purple crystal to Lonnie.

"A MacGuffin crystal? How did you..." Lonnie stopped as Coffee placed the broken halves of Larry in her hands. "Coffee...you know this can't bring *him* back, it can only–"

Coffee put a finger to Lonnie's mouth. "I'm aware. But maybe you can give someone else a fresh start..." Coffee looked up at one of Coffee Two's long arms attached to the ceiling.

"Who's this clown?" Coffee Two asked, obnoxiously.

Coffee smiled at Lonnie. "Goodbye, forreal this time." Coffee turned around.

"Where will you go?" Lonnie asked as the others were silent.

Coffee turned back and confidently said, "Strip club." They jettisoned through the wall, despite a perfectly good hole being mere feet away, and disappeared into space.

"I'm definitely not getting my security deposit back," Kale grumbled.

As this happened, Wixby and Lonnie's dad/Kale's therapist climbed through another hole. They stepped over the body of Evil Kale nonchalantly. "That was some quick thinking. You all make quite the team."

Kale turned to Lonnie's dad and smiled. "Someone told me that words were the most powerful weapon..."

Lonnie's dad squinted at him. "Yeah...so, when I said that, I thought you were also a magic-user..." Lonnie's dad muttered some dark incantations and a blast of energy shot from his mouth, creating yet another hole in the wall.

"Oh," Kale replied.

"It may have been a dumb idea, but it worked." Lonnie put an arm around Kale.

Before the two could get too romantic, Snacks also put an arm around Kale. "Hey, remember the time Kale kissed me?"

Kale sighed as Del leaned on Lonnie, and so began the slow zoom out that wraps up all adventures. But as the outro music swelled, it was cut short by a screech. And not the screech of a record scratch, but that of a bird.

Del had a moment of realization, "Oh, right, forgot about them..."

"About who?" Snacks asked.

At that moment, giant Space Eagles landed in front of the house. The magnificent birds bowed their heads, then looked around, a bit confused.

"Sorry, I forgot to text that we wrapped this up already! There's no fight anymore!" Del yelled.

"SCREECH!"

"Yes, I know you flew a long way."

"SCREECH!"

"Yes, I'm aware Space Eagles aren't aligned with anyone, so you choosing to support us in a battle is awe-inspiring and unexpected."

"SCREECH!"

Del sighed. "Yes, I'm aware you were supposed to show up when all hope was lost and turn the tide of battle."

"SCREECH!"

"Well, that's just uncalled for."

"SCREECH!"

"No, *YOUR* mother's a seagull!

"SCREECH!"

"If it's racist when I said it, it was racist when *YOU* said it!"

"SCREECH!"

"SCREECH!" Del and the largest eagle screeched at each other for another minute or so before the majestic, and slightly prejudiced, Space Eagles flew away.

"Well, that kinda ruined the happy ending," Del grumbled.

"Yeah..." Kale tapped his feet. "...Hey, why don't we do what we always do and listen to electro-jazz music?"

Everyone excitedly cheered and leapt in the air, freeze-framing while dope electro-jazz music played.

The End.

*In memory of all those who died because someone didn't do their dishes.*

# Epilogue

A uthor's note: we tried to get an 80s power ballad to play over the epilogue, but we *"couldn't secure the rights,"* and *"this is a book, so we don't need music. Who is this?"* But please, if you'll indulge this final request, put on some dope music as we wrap up our time together.

IN THE DAYS THAT FOLLOWED, SNACKS GOT SICK FROM TOUCHING THE doorknob. Kale made soup for him, and Snacks vowed never to touch a doorknob again.

The party of adventurers was able to harness the power of the portal and jump to a universe where Earth was still intact. Lonnie and Del stayed with Kale and Snacks while they fixed up their apartment...which coincidentally had also been destroyed in this universe.

Lonnie used the MacGuffin crystal to reanimate Larry, essentially rebooting him without any memories after being pulled from the stone. Larry and Coffee Two hit it off immediately.

Last the party heard of Coffee, they frequented a strip club for magical weapons called The Glistening Glaive.

Del was promoted to Director of All Falling Object Deaths and within a few years would be on the list of *10,000 Under 10,000 To Watch.*

She helped Kale secure a paid internship at Reapr. He later became a counselor for those who died due to a hero complex.

Snacks continued to date Revinath for a bit. She went from special guest star to full-time cast member, but unfortunately had to be cut from future installments due to scheduling conflicts.

Lonnie and Kale enjoyed their coffee date, but they're taking things slow...jeez, back off a bit, no need to rush into this.

Kale remembered to repay Lonnie eight dollars and to buy her a new coat.

Snacks made fun of Kale for kissing him to the point where it stopped being funny, but then it got funny again. Much to everyone's joy, he also stopped doing close-up magic.

Lonnie invented time travel or something.

Dog, the cat, got turned into a penguin. They still don't know how, but Dog seems to enjoy it much more.

Wixby eventually stumbled into the position of President of The Multiverse. He does a surprisingly good job and never Tweets anything racist.

They signed the Kraken up for CthulhuMatch, and it found a mythical beast that likes to hug as much as it does. They're both very happy now.

The four main characters went bowling once, but they were more interested in the monogrammed shirts.

Snacks kicked down the door hundreds, if not thousands, of times. However, the only time Kale tried it, it jostled the can holding up the shelf in Chapter 8. The whole thing toppled over and revealed a gun hung on the wall with the name *"Chekhov"* written on it.

\* \* \*

THE ADVENTURES CONTINUED. ON ONE SPECIFIC SUNDAY, THEY WERE ALL getting ready for their weekly session of family brunch and *Dungeons & Dragons*.

"Where's Kale? It's not like him to be late," Snacks wondered.

And at that very moment, Kale burst through the door. He had an eyepatch, but they were used to that by now. He wheezed and held out a paper bag.

The others looked around, a bit nervous. "What's wrong?"

Kale surveyed them with both panic and excitement. "I found it..." He caught his breath. "I found...The Everything Bagel."

The End
(For Real This Time)

# Postface

:)

Like this book? Find it in other universes under
these titles:

---

How To Fix An Uncomfortable Couch Filled With Portals

A Tale of Two Robots

Lonnie Quest

Hey Wasn't *The Office* Great?

A Love Ballad To *The Office*

I Wanted More Seasons Of *The Office* And Wrote A Whole Book To Cope
With The Gaping Hole It Left In My Heart

Why You Should Hug Sea Monsters

Basically Just A Worse Version of *The Hitchhiker's Guide to the Galaxy*

## Dedication & Acknowledgments

For my family, my friends, and my teachers, all of whom...held me back! Later suckers, seeya never!!!

...Just kidding, can you imagine?

Many amazing people contributed to this book, but I don't want to mention them by name in case they think they'll deserve a favor one day, so I will stick to those to whom I am legally obligated.

Tony Gangi took this story from a jumbled mess to a significantly less jumbled mess with an interesting theme and sense of pacing. His kind words were instrumental in making this the best story it can be.

The brilliant Erin Arata edited this and provided great insight into cat breeds. She did all the sentences good.

In all seriousness, the people in my life are the best sort of people. From those who raised me to those who lean into the bits, you make this world worth living in.

And a very special thanks to The Great Amoeba.

*This book will be given freely to any library that asks.*
*If you purchased this book, thank you for your support!*
*If you pirated it, no hard feelings. I hope it brought you joy!*

www.ingramcontent.com/pod-product-compliance
Lightning Source LLC
Chambersburg PA
CBHW051947170626
46808CB00007B/2515